Twenty Somethings
For Love or Ambition

SUDHĀM

Leadstart
INKSTATE

ISBN 978-93-5438-719-7
Copyright © Sudham Ravinutala, 2021

First published in India 2021 by Inkstate Books
An imprint of Leadstart Publishing Pvt Ltd

Sales Office:
119-123, 1st Floor, Building J2, B - Wing,
Wadala Truck Terminal, Wadala East,
Mumbai 400022, Maharashtra, INDIA
Phone: +91 96999 33000
Email: info@leadstartcorp.com
www.leadstartcorp.com

Disclaimer: The views expressed in this book are those of the Author and do not pertain to be held by the Publisher.

Editor: Vaibhav Pathare
Cover: Arijit Gupta
Layouts: Victor Patali

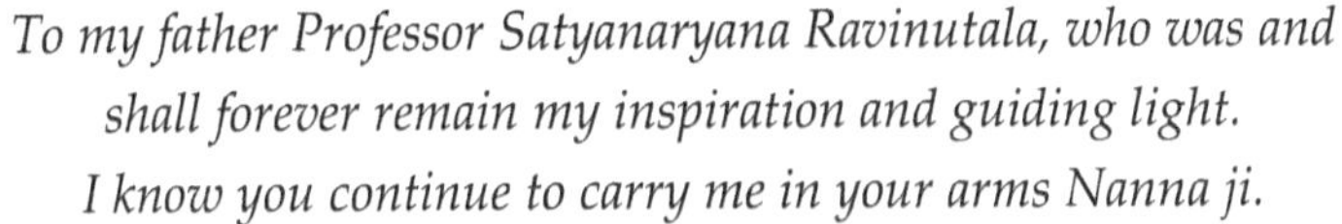

*To my father Professor Satyanaryana Ravinutala, who was and
shall forever remain my inspiration and guiding light.
I know you continue to carry me in your arms Nanna ji.*

*To my mother-in-law Smt. Raj Jain, one of the most selfless, caring,
and affectionate human beings I have known.
We miss you, Mummy!*

About The Author

Sudhām is a poet, marketer, and storyteller. He did his schooling in Delhi before moving out in pursuit of an engineering degree to Tumkur, a town in Karnataka, and later on to Mumbai where he completed his Post Graduate Diploma in Business Administration. He has been a part of the Indian corporate world for just over two decades now. In this duration, Sudhām has tried his hand at entrepreneurship and launched himself as an author with his work Eighteen-The End of Innocence in 2015. Now back into the corporate fold having had to beat retreat from entrepreneurship, he has steadfastly kept his writing dream alive.

A keen observer of people, culture, and customs, it is the nuance that piques Sudhām's interest. Years spent living in different cities of India at varying stages in life make fertile ground for his stories that delve into the grey areas of emotions and choices.

Twenty Somethings - For Love or Ambition is his second novel.

Sudhām lives in Suraj Kund near Delhi with his wife Surekha and daughters Mithila and Antara. He is currently associated with Luminous Power Technologies as Associate Vice President—Marketing and is championing the adoption of Solar Energy.

Sudhām can be reached at writetome@sudhaam.com and on leading social platforms with the handle **@sudhaam**. You can find more of Sudhām's writing (poetry, musings, and blogs on marketing) at www.sudhaam.com

Contents

Acknowledgements

Sitting down to write a note of acknowledgement is an onerous task for any author. The journey of publishing a book is long and arduous. From personalities that inspire the characters that an author builds, to incidents, events, and anecdotes that help weave the plot, there is help from so many quarters. Invariably a task that makes one reflect.

Writing has been a passion for as long as I can remember. I was introduced to books very early during my childhood courtesy of my father, himself an avid reader and an accomplished writer. It is he who has always inspired all my works. I also thank my mother and my teachers at school for the nurturing and encouragement that continues to this day. As I look back upon the past six years that this book has been in the making, I am grateful to the undermentioned.

Surekha, my wife, for her constant support and superfluous praise that always wrapped within it a critique of my writing. Thank you Surekha! I am an improved writer because of you.

My friends Ravi and Runa, for once again choosing to become soundboards for the countless plot directions I keep hurling at you.

Rishabh, for not holding back your criticism and thereby helping strengthen my conviction about the story that I set out to tell.

Aravind, for delving deep into the plot and giving valuable suggestions on making it tighter.

Ms. Teeshna Bahadur and Ms. Vanika Sinha for supporting me with invaluable case research.

My publishers Leadstart and the wonderful team led by Malini comprising Pooja, Trupti, and Ananya. My editor, Vaibhav Pathare, for putting in the hard miles over multiple rounds of editing and making the story more presentable.

Arijit, for yet another brilliant cover. You are a visual communicator par excellence. I am so thankful that you are my friend.

Finally, to the journey called life for planting these amazing stories around me. Some that I have told. Many that I am yet to tell!

PROLOGUE

Rishi rolled over and lit a cigarette. He sat up with his back resting against the head of the ornate bed. He took a long drag, the glow of the cigarette illuminating the dimly lit room. He was not always at home when it came to hotel rooms, but this was different. He was familiar with these surroundings. Rishi had been a regular guest at this particular hotel over the past one-year or so. The hotel management knew his preference and given a heads up, on more than a few occasions had ensured Room 304 was available to Mr. Hrishikesh Krishnamurthy.

"Pass me a drag," she said.

Rishi reached across the bed and handed her the cigarette.

"Careful!" he cautioned her, "You don't want to be making a habit out of it."

"I seem to have a habit of picking up 'habits' don't you think?" she said as she sat up, one hand holding on to the sheet. She flicked the ash into the tray by the bedside and handed back the cigarette to Rishi. The sheet had slipped in the process, exposing one of her breasts.

A wry smile broke on Rishi's face.

"It's not as though I haven't seen you," Rishi said, blowing out the smoke. "Never really understood why you women make so much effort to keep yourself 'covered'," he said gesturing closed quotes as he spoke.

"Precisely my point! Despite having seen them umpteen times, you insist on staring at them. They are just breasts, you know… and wipe that smirk off your face," Nitya said, clearly irritated. She had in the meantime, put on Rishi's vest that was lying on the floor next to her.

Nitya Ramanna was attractive. However, it was not her looks that had caught Rishi's attention. It was the way Nitya would blow off the hair that would fall over her face.

Rishi had known Nitya for a long time. The two were from the same engineering college.

~

Swami Hridayananda Institute of Technology or H.I.T (the 'S' had to be avoided in the abbreviated form for obvious reasons) was known for its rankers, not for its girls. Nitya though would have stood out in any crowd. Literally! She was tall for a girl, almost five feet nine, perhaps it was her Coorgi genes. She was fair, with a flawless complexion and a nose that seemed to have been chiselled to perfection. Nitya was an excellent speaker, a state-level volleyball player, a university medallist three years running, and if all that wasn't stand out, she was the only girl in H.I.T who rode a motorcycle. Not any motorcycle, mind you! A restored Yezdi!!

There were four batches of male engineering students who were vying for one glance from Nitya when Rishi had joined H.I.T. Nitya was already in her final year then. She was what they called in engineering college lingo, a 'super senior'.

It wasn't your typical love at first sight, at least not for Nitya. She wasn't looking for it then. That said, there was no way Rishi could have done anything about it—it happened!

Nitya was on a podium when Rishi first saw her. He still

remembered it was 'Technorama92', a technical symposium organised by the Computer Sciences Department and she was making a presentation on 'Remotely Operated Microprocessor Controlled Irrigation System'.

No! Rishi had no interest in the subject whatsoever. He was there for one simple reason. He had been hauled! All first-year students were 'fillers'. Their mandate was to not leave a single empty seat in the auditorium whenever important functions were being held by the institute.

They were also required to ask questions. Of course, the questions were handed to them by either the seniors or the lecturers. Rishi, was articulate, something that the lecturers had made note of. The folded chit that Rishi held in his hand had been slipped to him by Professor Venkatesh who was the Head of the Department of Computer Sciences.

"… and that's the reason we went for an 8085 chip despite the availability of the 8086. Does that answer your question?" Nitya leaned forward expectantly holding the lectern with both hands.

Rishi suddenly felt a sharp pain.

"Stop ogling *da*, just say thank you and sit the hell down!" It was Natarajan aka Nutty, his roomie, who had stomped hard on Rishi's foot.

"Hmm… yes, to a large extent. Thank you Nitya," Rishi pretended to have assimilated her response.

~

"Thank you! Your question helped us win," Nitya said as she walked up to the table Rishi was sitting at.   Rishi was in the canteen with some of his batchmates.

"You are in the first year aren't you? What's your name?" Nitya enquired holding out her hand.

"Hrishikesh, friends call me Rishi," he said shaking her hand. He knew the others sitting around the table were just happy that Nitya was standing there.

"Rishi it is then!" she said with a smile. "Well, see you around Rishi," she said as she walked away to join her friends. A beaming Rishi looked around as his classmates heaved a collective sigh.

"*Sariyaana figure*[1] *da... Lucky da nee,*" he heard one of the boys say woefully.

"She has a boyfriend *da*, his name is Dhananjay. He's that Arnold Schwarzenegger like fellow sitting to her right," one of the others said.

"He's from Delhi. Your senior only. Be careful!" someone warned.

The first-year students lived in constant fear of being summoned to a ragging session by their seniors. Everyone by default belonged to his or her respective state associations. The associations served as boundaries for whom you could rag or, who could rag you. Ragging, in that sense, was a federal subject.

"Guys relax!! She hasn't asked me out on a date! She just thanked me." Rishi said a trifle embarrassed with all the attention.

---

[1] Slang in Tamil often offensive. A term used to refer to a girl or a young woman. Equivalent of 'Hot Babe'.

As things turned out, Rishi did get along fabulously with both Nitya and Dhananjay or DJ, as he was popularly known.

Nitya was somewhat of a Midge to DJ's Moose like persona. Only, DJ was not dumb by any stretch of the imagination. Rishi had always liked them as a couple. Nitya was his favourite half, by far!

~

His train of thought ended abruptly. Years flew by in an instant as he got transported from the canteen in distant Mandya to the hotel room in Panvel, on the outskirts of Mumbai.

He heard Nitya step out of the bathroom.

She had just taken a shower. She was still as beautiful, as desirable. However, she no longer was the free spirit she once used to be. The passage of time had indeed taken its toll.

Rishi didn't like the fact that they had needed to sneak around. Nitya for sure didn't. They both knew it was a matter of time before reality rammed into them.

There was simply too much at stake. A lot many things to consider.

Love and ambition never did make for an easy choice!

MANDYA

~

The Journey Begins

I

"Getting into an engineering college is far easier than getting out of it. First-year was a cakewalk, a rehash of what you studied in school. Now that you have entered your home department you shall find out that your papa's money was only good enough to get you in. To get out you have to pass through me," the sadistic pleasure in the voice of K. Veera Aanjaneya, Professor of Electrical Engineering at Swami Hridayananda Institute of Technology was evident.

The not so veiled reference was to the 'payment seat' students. In other words, students who hadn't scored high enough in the entrance examinations to merit a seat, but those who by virtue of a separate higher fee structure had gained admission into an engineering college. Professor K. Veera Aanjaneya made no bones about his dislike for the payment seat system. He was known to set the bar in his course significantly higher.

"Darn! Satya was right *da*. We have taken the highway straight into hell!" Nutty muttered under his breath. Satyajit Sinha, Natarajan Iyer, Angshuman Lahiri, and Hrishikesh Krishnamurthy made the quartet that shared the hostel accommodation at H.I.T, Mandya.

It was a small batch of just twenty-one students who had opted for Electrical Engineering. Rishi and Nutty were amongst them.

"Those of you who paid attention in the Basics of Electrical Engineering course during your first year would be familiar with the transformer," the professor continued. "It is one of the most efficient electrical devices. For all of you in this department, I am that transformer! I will ensure that your potential is stepped up by the time you are on the other side. Welcome to the Electrical Engineering Department. I am K. Veera Aanjaneya, the Head of the Department. I am known as KVA," he concluded his address.

"Dude!! Transformer, KVA, step up, potential… get the pun?"

"Now you get it?? *Po da*[1] fucker… if only you had used your brains while taking the semester examinations you'd have cleared the Basics of Electrical Engineering," Nutty chided Rishi.

"Dude didn't KVA just say that he'll ensure our potential is stepped up," Rishi chuckled.

"You have a question, young man?" KVA's voiced boomed in the lecture hall. It took Rishi a couple of seconds to realise it was he who was being addressed.

"Er….no sir, not really," Rishi managed to mutter. "I was just telling my friend here that your initials are KVA and…" he replayed what he had told Nutty.

Nutty wasn't even looking at Rishi. From the corner of his eye, Rishi could actually see Nutty put some distance between them on the bench on which they were seated.

There are times in your life when you know in that very instant that you are making a mistake. You are aware that it's going to

---

[1] Tamil slang, the equivalent of "Get lost!"

stink yet, you succumb to the urge and let one rip!

"What's your name?" KVA asked.

"Hrishikesh Krishnamurthy sir," he said.

"Oh! So you are the one. I was very eager to meet the person who had made history."

"I don't understand, sir."

"It's the first time in our department that someone has topped and failed at the same time. You have the highest total marks amongst this class of twenty-odd students," KVA continued.

"Yet, you have failed to clear the Basics of Electrical Engineering, your chosen stream. Since you are that good at making the connection, for your sake son, I hope you make this one."

One could have heard a pin drop in that lecture hall, but Rishi could hear the roars of laughter that were being suppressed at that moment.

Smart, very smart!!

"As I said, papa's money was only good enough to get you in. To get out you have to pass through me." KVA's voice sounded even more sinister the second time around.

II

Swami Hridayananda Institute of Technology (H.I.T) was located in small-town Mandya, a hundred kilometres southwest of Bangalore, two-thirds of the way to Mysore.

Hrishikesh Krishnamurthy wasn't exactly elated when his candidature for Bachelor of Engineering in Electrical Sciences had been confirmed. The counsellor after three lengthy rounds of discussions and negotiations had finally offered Rishi a course of his choice. The only challenge was the fact that to get a course of his choice, Rishi needed to move to the payment seat category—a blow to his already dented pride.

Janardhanan Krishnamurthy, Rishi's father, was a Scientist by profession. He had moved to New Delhi from Madras in the early sixties when he had joined the National Physical Laboratory. Mr. Krishnamurthy was a man of humble beginnings. He had left home at an early age and had charted a career for himself as a scientist working by the day and earning his degrees by the night. His professional ascent was only partly due to his exceptional ability and was more because of his humility despite it.

Rishi, unfortunately, had inherited none of his father's exceptional abilities. That said, he did not inherit his mother's hard-working nature and meticulousness either. In genetic terms he was garbage! None of the good stuff had passed through the generational sieve. He was average, above at best.

Something that was a cause of worry for his parents.

Rishi wanted to change though. Not because of introspection or realisation therefrom but, for pride!

He was growing sick and tired of the open taunts of the well-meaning *paatis*[2] and *attais*[3] on either side of his family.

Every self-respecting Tamil Brahmin excels in academics and is culturally so evolved that he or she can start reciting *Thyagaraja Krithis*[4] in their sleep. Rishi drew a blank on both counts and comparisons with his father didn't help either.

Despite his cavalier dismissals of their comments, it bothered Rishi that his father had never commented on Rishi's abilities or as the case was, the lack of them.

No matter who or where or what the context Mr. Krishnamurthy would steadfastly say, "He's destined for bigger things."

Rishi wanted to live up to that. He did not know how he would eventually, but he thought getting an engineering degree would surely help begin that journey.

He had made Mr. Krishnamurthy gamble his provident fund savings to secure a course of his choice. A gamble, simply because even Rishi was not 100% certain about the why of his choice. He had heard someone say it was always better to go for one of the three "pure" engineering streams. Electrical Engineering or Mechanical Engineering in his mind seemed to be better choices as compared to Civil Engineering which reminded him of those hard-hatted men in Hindi movies who

---

[2] Tamil for Granny
[3] Tamil for Aunt
[4] Devotional compositions by Thyagaraja, 18th Century composer regarded as the Father of Carnatic music.

typically play the father or the brother of the protagonist. They would more often than not be bumped off by goons simply because they wanted to use the right mix of cement and *reth*[5]! Electrical was on offer and Rishi thought it prudent to take it. He had no intention of sharing his reasons with anybody. Least of all his father!

---

[5] A type of sand used in construction

III

Hrishikesh Krishnamurthy's first day at H.I.T was far from typical. One would normally expect an eighteen-year-old leaving home to stay in a hostel for the first time in his life to be a little nervous. Guarded for sure.

Rishi, on the contrary, was longing to embrace this promised freedom from playing the 'good boy'. The last couple of years in high school in the company of his buddies Abhi and Bhattu had been eye-opening in terms of the possibilities life as a young adult held! Very different indeed from the possibilities that his father had in mind for Rishi.

Mr. and Mrs. Krishnamurthy who had come down to help Rishi settle-in were bidding him goodbye. They were in his allotted hostel room. Rishi's parents were taking the train back to New Delhi later that evening.

"This is your first step towards building the rest of your life Rishi. Make sure you work hard son and destiny will smile at you," Mr. Krishnamurthy had said as he gave a hug to Rishi.

Mrs. Krishnamurthy's advice on the other hand had been less profound or shall we say more practical.

"Make sure you eat on time and get adequate sleep," his mother had said. "There will be no one to take care of your needs here. You have to take care of yourself."

"That reminds me Amma. Can you give me an extra hundred? I'll step out later this evening for dinner and see if I can pick up a few audio cassettes. Better than getting bored alone in the room."

His parents gave each other a look and obliged. Their son once again had evaded the profound and the practical with equal ease.

~

Rishi did step out of the campus later that evening but not before he had surveyed the hostel building. The hostel had a few students but wasn't full. He seemed to be one of the early boarders. Thus far he was the only one occupying the room. While the academic session started in a couple of days, the last rounds of counselling sessions were still on and that meant there were seats left to be filled in.

The room allotted to him and three other boys was at the far end of the corridor that led up from the building entrance. The hostel building itself was a three-storeyed quadrilateral, with the four sides comprising the four wings of the hostel block. Each wing had ten rooms on one floor, save the wing that faced Rishi's. It housed the mess or the cafeteria on the ground floor. The rooms were sandwiched between the common bathrooms and toilets on either end.

The central courtyard was almost the size of a football field. It was bordered by an unkempt hedge. There were badminton courts on the cafeteria side of the courtyard where some boys were playing.

The boys paused long enough to get a look at Rishi and continued playing as he walked past them.

"Later," he thought to himself. He was acutely aware that making friends and making them fast was the surest redemption from hostel boredom.

Having gone around the hostel block, Rishi stopped to read the announcements put up on the noticeboard at the entrance. Rishi skimmed through the notices. They contained information pertaining to key personnel and their telephone numbers, hostel and mess timings, etc. Rishi made a mental note to go through them in detail later.

His attention was drawn to the guard on duty who was putting up a fresh notification.

"What is it about?" he enquired.

The security guard did not respond. He had a bunch of sheets with him that needed to go up and he was trying hard to figure out a way to pin them all up.

"Here, let me help," Rishi said reaching out to collect the sheets from the guard. "Tell me what you need to be done."

The guard looked at Rishi for the first time during the entire conversation.

"*Student aa, ya roomu?*" he questioned in his accented, Kannada punctuated English.

"Yes, First Year, Triple E. Room number 20."

Offering help is perhaps the best way of breaking the ice and making friends. Rishi though unwittingly, had through his gesture made a friend in Basavaraj that evening. Ask any boarder and they'll tell you an obliging guard at the gates of a hostel is like pure gold!

The guard handed Rishi the bunch of papers. It contained the rooming details. Rishi stole a glance at the names against his allotted room as he pinned the sheets on the notice board.

As Rishi handed over the remaining board pins to the guard, he took out the key to his room from his pocket and gave it to him.

"I am the first one to occupy the room. I have used my lock. Please keep this spare key just in case."

~

He made the kilometre long walk to the campus main gate past the gymnasium, the auditorium, and the badminton and tennis courts. The campus itself was a miniature township spread over a hundred acres. It was perhaps one of the most beautiful and green campuses with streets lined with Ashoka trees and luscious groves, lawns, and thickets interspersed with the buildings.

The joy of listening to the sound of rustling leaves and the fragrant evening breeze seemed to have made his walk shorter. Rishi had reached the main gate already.

He hailed an auto.

IV

Mandya is your quintessential small town. The kind where nowhere is far from anywhere and everyone knows everyone. Rishi got a taste of it real early.

~

He had made his way to the liquor store. It was adjacent to the shop where he had picked up the audio cassettes he had set out to purchase. Once out of the campus he had duly boarded a *share-auto*[6] a concept he had no prior exposure to. The guard on duty at the main gate had suggested he take one when he'd enquired about the main market.

Rishi did not have to spend too much time picking up the cassettes. The store, surprisingly, had a much-updated collection of music. Posters of two of the recent releases which were on his mental list were proudly displayed on the store window and the albums promptly found their way into his shopping basket.

"Hey! You are the guy who has moved into Room No. 20! Aren't you?"

"Duh...yeah...well..." it took Rishi a while before he could overcome the initial embarrassment and respond. After all, getting spotted at the liquor vend on the very first day of college did have its connotations.

---

[6] A shared auto-rickshaw that typically plies a route and works on a hop on hop off concept. Popular in small town India.

"I'm Hrishikesh, you can call me Rishi. And you are?" he said, holding out his hand.

"Satyajit."

"Nutty."

"Angshuman."

"We are freshers too! Been here close to two weeks now. We were the first few to move into the hostel rooms," Satyajit said.

"Nutty here and I have been Volley Ball buddies since what… class ten?" Satyajit looked at Nutty for confirmation and got it promptly.

"First things first guys," said Angshuman, breaking the flow of introductions. "Presume the music was just an excuse to get some booze. What's your poison?"

"Yeah, join us. There's a permit room next door. Rum and Coke good with you?" Satyajit regained control of the conversation.

"Well…" Rishi trailed off.

"Commmme *da*…" Nutty put his arm around Rishi. The decision was made.

Rishi knew that alcohol made people shed inhibitions, but this was the first time someone was shedding them on his behalf. That too without a single drop being consumed. He decided to go with the flow.

Better than drinking alone.

As Humphrey Bogart put it in *Casablanca*, this was the beginning of a beautiful friendship.

V

It wasn't long before Rishi had convinced Satya, Nutty, and Oggy to move into Room No. 20. The boys had discovered common interests and similar backgrounds over a bottle of Old Monk XXX Rum that they ended up polishing between them.

Nutty incidentally had also chosen Electrical Engineering as his specialisation. Satya had opted for Mechanical Engineering whilst Oggy had gone with Chemical.

Satya was an athlete, and it showed. He was tall, perhaps a shade over six feet. His father, like Rishi's, was a scientist and worked for the Indian Institute of Science in Bangalore. His parents hailed from Sitamarhi District in Bihar and had settled in Bangalore during the late sixties. Satya courtesy being brought up in Bangalore was fluent in Kannada and could easily pass off as a local—an advantage in the H.I.T world, where ragging was part of a fresher's daily routine.

Add Nutty to the mix and it was adequate protection for Oggy and Rishi, who were both from Delhi.

Natarajan was stocky and muscular. His perennially bloodshot eyes and flowing moustache, to which he gave a constant twirl, were his signature. Nutty was a man of few words. His reactions and responses would normally be in monosyllables. His arms though were far more expressive. A firm handshake, a quick punch, an arm-twist, or a tight hug were way more forthcoming from good ole Nutty. Not only did Nutty believe in the prudent use of the spoken word, he believed in the economy of movement as well. You could trust him to come up with a method that involved the least effort on his part for doing, or rather not doing anything.

"I am a good manager *da*..." he would often quip, drawing instant ire from his roommates.

It didn't take Satya, Nutty, and Rishi long to figure out that Oggy was the most intelligent of the four. While Satya and Rishi were on the verbose end of the spectrum with Nutty on the silent end, Oggy was the one who chose his moments to speak, invariably wisely. He was an extremely good listener and someone who could put across his point of view in a very clear, concise, at times even blunt manner. Oggy was no nonsense, no pretence; not a people person.

At times when Oggy was not in the room, Satya would often wonder aloud and with sincerity as to what he and the others had done to have been blessed with Angshuman Lahiri as their friend and roommate. Oggy had very quickly slipped into the role of their time and conscience keeper.

However, no amount of respect or liking for each other prevented the boys from taking a dig.

"Can you believe it? This bugger got a letter within two days of moving into the hostel!"

"Not to forget the rose-scented envelope it came in. Who wouldn't have wondered?" Nutty added.

"As dim-witted as the two of you are, you assumed it had to be a girlfriend."

It was indeed a letter from a girl! Oggy was the pen-friend sorts. The lone pink envelope with the name Angshuman Lahiri calligraphically written on it had caught Satya's eye. He took it upon his person to deliver the letter to its intended recipient.

Satya and Nutty ganged up and knocked on Oggy's door, pretending to be seniors. They made Oggy read the letter aloud four or five times, each time having him intersperse each sentence with a limerick.

"Oh, shut up! Admit that we had you shitting bricks. One look from Nutty was enough to make you succumb to our demands."

"Bastards!"

~

Taking each other's trip was a standard pastime in Room No. 20. The constant war of wits had the four pairing up and combining with and against one another. They had something special going and acknowledgement from the rest of the hostel world wasn't far away.

Room No. 20 soon became the hub. The de facto common room. The boys didn't seem to mind at all!

VI

The first-years at H.I.T were a mixed batch. Students would take up their respective streams of specialisation during the second year.

The various departments of the institute would from time to time, organise special events. These events were designed in part to involve the first-year students by giving them a preview of each of the specialisation streams. The methods adopted were paper presentations, technical quizzes, panel discussions, and guest lectures.

The University followed a semester system and the odd semester had just ended. The semester-end examinations were followed by a short one-week break, barely sufficient for one to go home and come back.

Rishi along with Angshuman and a few more from their batch had booked their return tickets together.

For someone like Rishi, most of the break was spent making the 47-hour-a-side train journey to Delhi and back. Many students would gladly have extended the break, but the upcoming semester was dotted with 'events'. The even semesters were eagerly awaited and the excitement was palpable across not only batches of students but the teaching staff as well.

While the freshers viewed it as the beginning of some extra-curricular activity and a sort of rite of passage, the seniors loved putting the various events together. H.I.T was one of the few institutions that conducted such events and at a significant scale. Participation and coming out on top was prestigious as far as the participating institute was concerned. As for the students, they were more than happy pocketing the cash rewards!

The Computer Sciences Department of the college was the first off the blocks with Technorama. The marquee event was an intercollegiate Technical Paper Presentation. The event was restricted to those in the final year of engineering studies. The draw for the first-year students was a technical quiz. Rishi, an avid quizzer, had teamed up with Oggy.

~

"So? Did you guys find time to prepare?" Nutty asked excitedly.

They had just boarded the passenger train to Mandya, the last couple of hours before they reached their hostel rooms. Nutty and Satya had joined Rishi and Oggy at the Bangalore station.

"Barely. But I am not worried." Oggy replied confidently. "The other teams are just there for making up the numbers. Rishi and I were the only ones to register voluntarily. Besides, there's no real preparation one can do for a Tech Quiz."

"Here," said Satya offering the *paneer* rolls his mother had packed. "Let's team up and beat the shit out of these overconfident Delhi boys," he winked and said to Nutty.

"Overconfident my ass!" Rishi said reacting to Satya's jibe. "This silly Bong didn't allow me a single moment to myself during the entire train journey! He has been throwing questions at me from some goddamn quiz book he got his hands on."

"You'll be thanking me when we hold the trophy and receive that winner's cheque," Oggy said.

"Which of course shall immediately be utilised and well! Cheers!" Satya said clinking his roll with Nutty and Rishi.

During the remaining part of the journey, the boys exchanged happenings of the week gone by and soon found themselves unpacking in their room.

In no time, their room was back to being the common room. Pretty much everyone coming back from the holidays dropped in for a hello, a *by-two-chai*[7] chat, or a quick smoke.

You could feel the energy on the campus. It was in large measure, driven by the impending 'fest' season.

~

Rishi had settled in well. His roomies were a good lot, a fabulous mix of having fun when you can and paying attention to studies when you must.

Rishi was looking forward to the upcoming semester. Something told him that this one was going to be special. How? He didn't know, neither care, but special it was going to be!

---

[7] Colloquial usage especially in parts of Karnataka meaning a single cup of tea that's split and shared by two. Viewed as a smart buy since you pay half the price but usually are served more than half a cup! At times, even three-fourth!

VII

Oggy's confidence bore him out and his mini prediction did come true. It was Rishi's presence of mind though that took them over the line in what was a nail-biting final round of the quiz. A dream come true or a nightmare depending on which side you end up on. Clearly, it was the former as far as Rishi and Oggy were concerned.

The nature of the win did a couple of things for Rishi. It brought him instant adulation from an entire batch of first-year students.

The good part about being the first one to do anything is the fact that even if someone else comes around and does it bigger or better than you did, your name is still eternally connected with the event.

Rishi and Oggy were the first team from H.I.T in twenty years of Technorama history to win the quiz. The manner in which they did and the fact that they were a couple of first-year students who beat a largely 'senior' competition from sixteen participating institutes made the win legendary.

The second thing that happened and this one more equitably and in a positive manner of speaking, was that Rishi and Oggy came into notice of the college professors and also some seniors.

~

"Tu Dilli ka hai na?"

Rishi turned around unsure whether the question had been directed at him. It was the day after their win. Rishi had been expecting some kind of recognition, even admiration but the tone of the question was sans any of the two. Rishi did not know how to react to a random question about his hometown from a random guy.

Rishi happened to be walking past the large seminar hall. Nutty was with him.

The boy who had called out to him was sitting on a motorcycle. He had his brows raised in anticipation of a response from Rishi.

"Yes, I am."

"Think I saw you in the South Extension market last week. Were you there?"

Rishi nodded. With the threat of ragging looming large he wasn't sure in which direction this conversation was headed. He looked at Nutty for some kind of support, there was none to be found.

"Who was the girl with you? Your girlfriend?"

This was getting sticky.

"Machan,[8] we need to change into regular wear and rush back. You better hurry." Nutty turned around and started walking away.

If ever, there had been a perfect time to speak this was it. Nutty

---

[8] Tamil for brother-in-law. Colloquially used to address friends in South India, esp., in the city of Chennai.

had delivered the line in such a matter-of-fact manner that even the boy on the motorcycle was stumped. Perhaps he wasn't expecting the implied "Get on with it!" kind of admonishment in Nutty's tone or his nonchalance.

Nonetheless, he let it pass. Rishi was only too eager. The conversation had ended.

He caught pace with Nutty who hadn't bothered to check whether and if at all Rishi was with him. He seemed lost in thought.

"Close call," Rishi said heaving a sigh of relief.

"I don't think he meant to rag you," said Nutty pronouncing his verdict.

"What makes you say that?"

"Instinct."

Rishi knew Nutty enough to understand that no further response could be elicited from him on this matter.

Rishi was itching to talk about the incident but to his disappointment, neither Satya nor Oggy were in the room. They quickly changed into regular wear from the workshop overalls that they were wearing. Not another word was spoken.

~

They were back in the seminar hall now. On their way in, one of the professors had called Rishi to the side and tasked him with asking a question.

He was a 'plant'. A popularly known and even accepted tactic deployed in technical symposiums and paper presentations by the participants. Sometimes, even the judges. Depending on which one of the two deploys the tactic, the plant is required to ask a question that is designed to either stump the presenter or offer a juicy half-volley that can be hit out of the park. Rishi was pretty sure he was the latter. This was their turf as far as the symposium was concerned and he was more than happy to help the home contestant win.

VIII

"She is the one!" Rishi felt a tap on his shoulder. It was Professor Venkatesh. "Pay attention and make sure you put your hand up as soon as she concludes." Rishi nodded his head in acknowledgement.

The presenter in question, in the meantime, had made her way to the podium.

Man she's pretty!

Rishi paid attention all right, but it wasn't to the paper being presented. He just happened to find the presenter worthier!

She had introduced herself as Nitya Ramanna. She was a final year Computer Science major. Her paper presentation was punctuated with a peculiar mannerism that Rishi found extremely cute! Nitya had short hair. From where Rishi was seated, he could see that she had used several clips to hold her hair back. Yet, there was an errant wisp that had managed to escape. Nitya, whenever she could afford a pause in her paper reading, would give a quick blow through the corner of her lips to prevent the wisp from falling over her eye. She could have used her hands too, but she didn't, perhaps wouldn't. The only attention he paid during the entire presentation was to count the number of times Nitya blew at her hair.

"...with that, I open the floor for questions."

Rishi, fortunately, remembered that he was to raise his hand. He did!

He had to wait his turn till the judges had finished their questions. Rishi did not have the foggiest idea of what transpired.

"Could you please tell us the reason you chose to use the 8085 microprocessor chip for your system despite the availability of the 8086 chip? The 8086 chip offers Instruction Queues, Pipelining, and Multiprocessing Support that clearly would benefit better functioning."

Rishi had managed to get a glance at the chit that Professor Venkatesh had handed to him. He spewed out the content verbatim.

Nitya placed both her hands on the lectern, took a deep breath while assimilating the question, puffed out at her hair again, and began her response.

Rishi was smitten!

~

Later that afternoon, while Rishi and a bunch of friends were in the college canteen Nitya walked up to Rishi and thanked him. The pleasure of the first introductions was short-lived. His friends had just informed him that Nitya had a boyfriend. That in itself was not the problem. Her boyfriend was the senior who had stopped Rishi and Nutty earlier and he was at that moment walking towards them!

"Hello Rishi! I am Dhananjay."

"Hrishikesh...Rishi." he responded hesitantly.

"Sorry, I got lost in small-talk earlier. I was supposed to brief you regarding the question you were to ask. Anyway, all's well that ends well."

Rishi managed a smile. Nutty was right indeed. Dhananjay was not trying to rag him.

"Hey! We are heading into town to celebrate Nitya's win. Why don't you join us?" Rishi's hand was still locked in a firm handshake with Dhananjay.

"Thank you Dhananjay sir! May be some other time." Rishi added the 'sir' to Dhananjay's name as was the custom. Juniors were supposed to.

"I insist," Rishi felt Dhananjay's grip firm up, "and I hate this sir business. Not required. I prefer Dhananjay or DJ."

Rishi saw Nitya from the corner of his eye. She was looking over her shoulder, waving her hand asking Rishi to join them.

For the record, Rishi was too scared to refuse.

IX

It was his first time riding pillion on a motorcycle with a girl. To say the least, it was an awkward ride. Not because Rishi was too much of a man, but practically so. Rishi would have tried at least three different places to get a comfortable grip on Nitya's Yezdi D250 while riding. He tried the backrest, the metal grip above the rear shockers, and the backrest extensions just below the seat.

"You can place your hands on my shoulders," Nitya said. She was amused, she had been seeing Rishi fidget in the rear-view mirror. "You see around the waist is reserved for DJ," she chuckled. "Try if you want to at your peril."

Given his state of infatuation, Rishi did honestly consider the option. He concluded that hands on Nitya's shoulders would be more 'appropriate'.

A normal ride into town would have been a short one. But, Nitya, DJ, and four of their batchmates were bikers. For them, a ride into town meant a ride around it first!

It was a different high for Rishi. He thoroughly enjoyed the ride that was followed by hot cups of tea and *bajjis*[9]. The short college life till then had mostly been about lengthy debates or dumb charades or rounds of rum and Coke.

---

[9] A deep fried savoury snack made of vegetables dipped in chickpea batter typically served with a chutney. The South Indian equivalent of a *pakora*.

Rishi did feel a twang of jealousy when he saw Nitya and DJ enjoying a moment at the *tapri*[10]. He could sense that they got along fabulously.

Get over it!

~

He rode with DJ on the way back. The conversation outside the seminar hall that had abruptly ended was revived.

"So? Who was that girl you were with in Delhi? Someone special?" DJ shouted over his shoulder.

"Not really," Rishi said avoiding an answer as much as giving one. It did not matter. This was a part of his life he had not shared with anyone yet in H.I.T. DJ surely wasn't going to be the first.

"*Accha!* Only after *daaru*[11] is it? You should drop by my room sometime. I have some Fenny and port wine that we picked up on our last ride to Goa."

Riding pillion behind Nitya and DJ was a study in contrast. Nitya was focussed on the road, there was little or no talk during the ride. Which incidentally, was just perfect as far as Rishi was concerned since he had his thoughts for company.

With DJ, it was a whole different experience. He was not conscious of the bike. It was as though the motorcycle was an extension of his body and riding it came with an ease that was similar to walking. His constant talk didn't seem to compromise his skill. And boy, could he talk!

---

[10] A shanty tea-stall that is typically located close to college campuses, bus-stands, railway stations etc.
[11] Booze

Rishi was leaning forward with his head over DJ's shoulder during the entire ride. If only Nitya had spoken half as much, the smile on Rishi's face would have been around even longer.

By the time they were back DJ had told and found out about where they went to school, what sport they played, great places to eat back in Delhi, favourite music, etc. There was also a part where the girls they had dated came up. This time, DJ stayed clear of questions.

X

"You do know that she's in love with someone else, don't you?"

Satya and Rishi had gone for an early breakfast at the *tapri*. They were sipping tea while waiting for their sandwiches to arrive.

"It's not like that."

"Don't go down this path Rishi." There was some amount of anger but mostly frustration in Satyajit's voice.

~

Rishi had been spending a lot of time in the company of Nitya. Not always alone though.

The past few months had been dotted with multiple extra-curricular events both within and outside the college. Rishi and Nitya were invariably participants and kept bumping into each other. There was a fair sprinkling of victories that needed celebration too.

To be honest, it was not just Nitya and Rishi but the extended group of friends that had started meeting regularly. Satya, Oggy, Nutty, and DJ were all a part of this group and there were more. About twenty of them! This was perhaps the first time in the history of H.I.T that such a tight bond and friendship had existed across the four years of engineering batches.

They were the regulars who would participate in the 'cultural' activities as they were known. It was not surprising at all when most of them found a spot on the committee for cultural affairs that was announced by the Chairman.

It was only a week ago that they had participated in a festival at Manipal. The event, a grand three-day affair, was a revelation of sorts for the ten-member team that H.I.T had sent. The prize money for each of the events was a feature attraction. The group, therefore, had decided to participate in some non-standard events as well. The schedule was already known and the planning for the teams and partners was completed during the overnight bus journey from Mandya to Manipal. A small contingent meant that people had to team up and participate in multiple events to increase the chances of winning anything. The regular quiz pair of Oggy and Rishi was therefore split into two teams. Rishi was to pair up with Nitya while Oggy was with Satya. Rishi and Nitya also happened to be a part of the dumb charades team along with another girl who was from the second year.

Rishi sat next to Nitya during the bus ride. The stated pretext, not that anybody had expressed reservations, was preparation.

"Great! I'll sit with you guys!" said the girl inviting herself to sit next to them. That is exactly what they did for the first hour or so before their teammate dozed off.

~

The tea that Usha, as Rishi found out her name was, had during the short-break in the bus journey didn't help. After boarding the bus again, she requested a swap for the window seat with Rishi. Once seated, she rolled up her *dupatta* into a ball, put it between her head and the windowpane, wished Nitya and Rishi goodnight, and promptly resumed her slumber.

It surely was more than filter coffee as far as Rishi and Nitya were concerned, that helped them stay awake. The two spent all night talking.

They were quiet enough not to disturb the nighttime peace that had descended and loud enough for them to hear one another. A significant challenge considering the rattle and hum of the bus and the loud asynchronous snoring around them.

They talked about growing up. She told him about her family and its military lineage, about her sister, being raised virtually as boys, her passion for bikes, her plans to pursue further studies abroad, her relationship with DJ, and a whole lot more.

Rishi was mostly the listener that night. He would not have uttered a word had it not been for Nitya asking him closed-ended questions. Rishi told her about his travails and how he ended up with Electrical Engineering at H.I.T.

Before long it was daybreak!

XI

On reaching their destination and having completed the registration formalities, the H.I.T team had chosen to have breakfast at the North Indian Mess, one of the many on Manipal Campus.

"I was knocked out cold last night!" said Usha who was seated across the dining table. "Do fill me in on the codes that you guys have decided upon."

Rishi looked at Nitya, a sheepish smile broke on both their faces.

"Oh! Don't worry it shall take all of five minutes," Nitya said responding to Usha's query.

That was exactly how long Nitya took to explain the dumb charade codes. Fortunately for the three of them, most of the codes they intended to use were standard and the syncing up helped. They practiced for about an hour and this time made a few codes along the way.

The quiz prelims were scheduled later that afternoon. They were left with just enough time to go to their rooms and freshen up.

Nitya announced she would be staying in her sister's room in the medical college campus a short walk away. Satya tagged along to meet his girlfriend who too was studying medicine.

~

The quiz prelims were tough. Every right answer was worth its weight in gold. There were fifty questions in the written round of the quiz. The best team got only twenty-one of them right. Out of the six teams to be chosen for the final round, two were tied on nineteen and one each, on eighteen and seventeen. As luck would have it, the two teams from H.I.T were tied for the sixth spot on the finals. Both the teams had ended up with sixteen right answers each.

The rules called for an open tiebreaker. Satya, Oggy, Rishi, and Nitya got into a huddle while the organisers pulled out a tiebreaker question.

"Guys, either way, it's only one team that is going through," Satya said. "I suggest we decide amongst the four of us and give a walk-over to the other team. At least we come out on top psychologically!"

"Or…" Nitya said wondering aloud. The others waited for her thoughts to assimilate.

"… we propose to them that one member from each of the teams goes forward forming a new team. Bet they wouldn't have a scenario where participating teams from the same college have teams that are tied," Nitya continued.

The boys found Nitya's suggestion worth consideration. The question though was which two.

"Oggy, Rishi…I think it's best if you guys team up again. It's our best shot!" Satya said voicing his vote and sort of verdict since it had Nitya's nod.

It seemed logical. Between the two teams, with Rishi and Oggy combining, they had twenty-three questions correct. Their combined capabilities could actually have put them in the first position!

The four of them made their proposal to the organisers. Nitya was right! They didn't have a clause for this peculiar situation and consented to the 'merger'. The other contesting teams, however, objected.

After a second round of deliberations it was decided that Rishi and Nitya would step back. Rishi wasn't too happy about it but Nitya prevailed.

XII

"**O**h! Come on!! Stop sulking! Don't be such a baby!" Nitya admonished Rishi. Rishi and Nitya were sitting outside the hall where the final round of the quiz was to be held.

"We should have gone for the tie-breaker question. The quiz is my primary event and I don't even make it to the final round?!" Rishi lamented.

"You probably would have! Maybe even have won the quiz. I take the blame as the captain of the contingent. I should not have split the teams in the first place! Having done that, there was no way I could have suggested that you and I go through. So, if there's anyone you need to be miffed with, it's me."

"I get that. I would much rather have won the tie-breaker," said Rishi looking up.

Nitya was now standing up. Her hands were placed purposefully on her waist. Rishi figured he was one utterance away from getting whacked by Nitya. What caught his attention though, was how she had the sun behind her, and the gentle breeze ruffling her hair. He couldn't see her face, just her silhouette. In that moment the anger and frustration of not making it to the final round of the quiz melted away.

"Let me make it up to you," Nitya said bringing Rishi back from his reverie. "Our next event together is dumb charades which is not until tomorrow. The rest of our day today is open. Let's take a ride to the beach. You can sulk all you want. The sunset at Malpe is breath-taking!"

Rishi held out his hand. Nitya pulled him up, literally and metaphorically.

~

Malpe Beach was just a short ride away. Twenty minutes or thereabouts. The Kinetic Honda Nitya's sister had, was at Nitya's disposal for the length of their stay. It was being put to use for a noble cause. That of cheering Rishi up!

"Wanna try?"

"No way! I am not good with two-wheelers."

Once again, it was Rishi riding pillion. He was beginning to enjoy these rides.

They hit the beach straight away. It was just after noon and despite the favourable weather, there weren't many people to be seen. The sky was dotted with clouds, the white cottony ones that hang high above. It was the second week of November and the tropical sun had lost its bite over the longish monsoon that had ended a few weeks ago. The sea breeze made for a pleasant walk and of course, more talk!

It was Rishi who spoke for the most part this time adding a few anecdotes along the way. It was a freer-flowing and a less dumbstruck Rishi on display. Nitya burst out laughing when Rishi termed himself 'genetic garbage'. She of course found his reasons for deciding on the course bizarre.

Talking about education and career got Nitya started. Not

about herself, but about DJ.

"He just seems to have one purpose in life," she stopped, stood still for a second and pointed towards herself with both hands, and said, "Me!"

"Isn't that a compliment?"

"No Rishi! You don't understand!" There was angst in her voice.

"One cannot lead life like a paper bag whose ascent and direction are determined by the gust of wind that blows it around."

This is your chance. Go for the girl!!

 "Come on! I think you are being too harsh on poor DJ. The guy loves you for God's sake!" said Rishi instead, dismissing the thought.

 "Yes, I know! And, it feels wonderful to be loved. The trouble is, we can't keep riding around on motorcycles forever. We are almost out of engineering college and we still don't know what our future is. Not even whether we have each other in it. Believe me, I have tried talking to him. Not once has he taken me seriously."

They stopped.

The setting sun had painted the sky with myriad shades of orange and red. The sun itself had turned fluorescent orange. At the end of the horizon, the sea had taken on the colour of the sky above. One could see blue-black darkness waiting on the edges to envelope the sky. A few fishing boats making their return to the shore made the picture perfect.

Breath-taken they watched the sea gobble the giant ball of fire. It must have been instinctive because neither one was conscious of the fact that they were holding hands.

XIII

"Let's do it!" There was excitement in Satya's tone. The students of H.I.T had been participating in various college festivals across the country and had been winning on a fairly regular basis.

The boys, in their usual gatherings in Room No. 20, had started discussing the possibility of organising an intercollegiate cultural festival of their own. The concept had found favour amongst a few of the students from the senior batches too.

About twenty of them showed up for the cross-batch huddle at the rooftop of the first-year boys' hostel. The word about the meeting had been spread to reach the ears of 'like-minded people'.

There were a few new faces and pleasantly so. Rishi and Satya were in the middle of the huddle. They had just finished making their pitch. The composition of the huddle was, by and large, the cultural committee that had been appointed by the college authorities. Which inherently, should have been a good thing, but the spirits were not as high as they had hoped for.

"Well… you can give it a shot if you want," said one voice.

"We've suggested it before but nothing has ever come out of it. You are not the only guys who thought of this," said another.

"We definitely aren't the first ones to come up with the idea.

But we shall be the last!" Rishi said emphatically trying to mask his disappointment with positive speak.

"Yes! We will be the ones to organise the first-ever cul-fest[12] at H.I.T. History beckons guys!" said Satya taking a cue from Rishi.

"Here's what we propose."

Over the next fifteen minutes, Satya and Rishi took the group through the possible next steps on how they could all work together to sell the idea to the college authorities.

They had a plan that could address the primary hurdle, budgets. The two with help from a few of the others had been collecting information on associated costs and had built an estimate. Friends and friendships made in different engineering colleges over the past few months of attending intercollegiate competitions had come in handy.

"Sponsorships are key. We can also get substantial money if we sell stalls."

"You guys think brands are going to queue up for you?" quipped one.

Negativity reared its head again for a wee moment. Fortunately, the naysayers were a reducing tribe.

"I can try asking my father, he heads marketing for a popular apparel brand and I know for a fact that they associate with college festivals," one of the third years said.

"True. My local guardian has a motorcycle dealership in Mandya. Guessing he would be interested," added another.

---

[12] Colloquial. College lingo for Cultural Festival.

Belief is a wonderful thing. If you have it, you can get what you don't have.

The gathering dispersed. However, not before deciding that a representative group would meet the Director of the institute.

The rooftop meeting had concluded on a positive note.

Satya put his hand up. They high fived.

It was early days yet but things were about to change at H.I.T. Both Satya and Rishi knew it.

XIV

Weeks of intense preparation, heated arguments, the hunt for elusive sponsors followed the meeting with the Director of the institute.

He was seated at the end of a rather funnily done up office room. Unlike most offices, the occupant had his back to the entrance. One had to go around the room to make their presence known. To make things worse, the room itself was a long hall and there was an entire length of a boardroom table to contend with.

Satya and Rishi were accompanied by Jazz, a supportive senior. Jazz, whose actual name was Jayashankaran was a second-year student. Jazz had found strong allies in Satya and Rishi. He had been pushing the powers that be to host a cultural festival at H.I.T for more than a year now.

Jayashankaran truly believed that he belonged to another place and time, the reason he preferred being addressed by his self-given nickname 'Jazz'. The place specifically was the 'US of A'. He would often be seen walking around the campus with the prospectus of some US-based university or the other. He would also have a host of related documentation about where to stay, how to secure an assistantship etc. Apart from harbouring dreams of studying in the US, Jazz had one other mission. He wanted to make "(S).H.I.T cool!", as he would pun every so often.

Standing at the far end, they were waiting for the wise men i.e. the Director, the Chairman of the Cultural Committee, and the Dean of Student Affairs to pronounce their verdict.

The three boys had taken the senior troika through an elaborate plan. Rishi thought they had prepared and presented well. They had covered pretty much all bases. The list of institutes, the events, the logistics for boarding and lodging of the participants and all of that rolled into a tidy account of expenditure. They had one trump card though that they had not played yet.

"We do not have the funds for this kind of event," the Chairman began.

"… however," he said stopping to take a significantly pregnant pause, "we could approach our friends in the industry for sponsorships."

"Why to burden the children with unnecessary work Professor," the Director said breaking his silence.

"I shall visit the *matha*[13] and seek support from Guruji. I am positive he shall support this."

The boys hadn't expected this at all. Their trump card was the sponsorship interest that they had already generated.

"Sir, with your permission…" Satya interjected, giving Rishi a nudge imploring him to join in.

The Director nodded his go-ahead.

"We have informally been discussing the possibility of sponsorship with a few businesses…" Satya continued, still hesitating.

---

[13] Kannada word of Sanskrit origin meaning monastery.

"… and we have been able to generate interest too!" Rishi chipped in excitedly.

They'd developed a good partnership in quick time. Satya and Rishi could catch on to each other's thoughts and build on it. Rishi did exactly that.

"That's good! I do not mean to suppress your enthusiasm," the Director said having given a patient listening once again. "One thing we engineers understand better than others is proof of concept and we must use it to our advantage."

The three boys looked at each other befuddled. They weren't sure of the direction in which the discussion was headed.

"Do it with the resources the institute makes available for you. Organise it well, prove the concept, and batches for years to come shall thank you. What shall follow the event's success is not just sponsorships. This event can bring us untold benefits in the form of reputation, pedigree, and even industry interest in the form of recruitments."

"I am going to request Guruji for three lakhs." The Director said to the Chairman and the Dean.

He looked at the boys and said, "Gentlemen! I believe you also have a name for the event."

"We wanted to name the festival Melange," Rishi said finding his voice first. Satya and Jazz were still coming to terms with the joy of what they had just heard.

"Signifies the coming together of multiple talents and also students from across the country," Satya added.

Jazz added some drama to the moment by pulling out a banner

with "Melange '93" written on it. He and Rishi had spent hours in the Computer Lab, first stealthily installing a banner making software and then taking a print-out on the already overworked dot-matrix printer. He seemed to have put in the colours by himself. There had been no previous discussion about the stunt. The other two boys had been taken by surprise too.

"You know *Mele-anga* has a meaning of its own in Kannada." The Dean, who'd remained silent all this while spoke up. "Loosely translated it would mean upper body part." He started laughing only to realise no one else had joined him.

"*Yenu matadta idira Saar*[14]?!" The Chairman jumped in to rescue the boys and the discussion. "Every name or word can be contorted that way. Let's support the boys," he said, the tone of his voice almost admonishing the Dean.

"Why not just call it H.I.T Intercollegiate Cultural Festival?" the Director said with all seriousness.

"Sir, all the festivals have a name and it is important to have a simple one, we do have a few back-up options," Jazz blurted. The other two nodded.

"Why to add to the confusion? Melange has a good ring to it. I recommend we stick with it," the Chairman advised. "Just make sure no other festival has that name," he pronounced, clearly seeking closure with caution.

"We already did sir!" Rishi said confidently. "The proposal has an annexure that contains a list of the most well-known college festivals across the country. The name Melange seems to be available."

---

[14] Kannada for "What are you saying?" Typically used in a rhetorical sense.

"Even if it is taken. We shall make it synonymous with H.I.T. sir!" Satya added.

"Melange it is then! Start your preparations."

XV

"We are a team again and you are riding with me to Tumkur tomorrow," there was an indisputable authority in her tone.

"Good! Did I hear you say riding?!"

"Yes! Captain's orders."

"May I at least register protest?"

"Okay, this can go on forever. I am stepping in for Oggy. You and I are going to partner for the quiz at SIT, Tumkur."

"Something tells me this has nothing to do with Oggy's inability to attend."

"Pack light. Nothing more than a haversack. I'll pick you up from the hostel in the morning. 6 AM sharp. Trust me it shall be a day you'll remember… for a long time to come," she added sensing Rishi's apprehension.

~

Rishi didn't have to wait very long the next morning. Nitya, true to her word, was there sharp at six.

"Wear these," she said as she handed Rishi a jacket and a helmet to wear.

"It is DJ's, bound to be a bit loose for you." She chuckled as Rishi slipped into the clearly oversized jacket.

"Hey! Wish me first!!" Nitya said just as Rishi was about to take the pillion.

"Okay, why do I sense that there is a joke out there and it's on me?" Rishi threw his hands up in the air somewhat exasperated.

"It's my birthday today silly. DJ is out playing a tournament and I wanted to spend it with someone special."

Rishi felt like scum.

Recover! You dickhead!

"Well then! A birthday wish ought to be accompanied by a hug," Rishi said with his arms wide open. He wasn't too pleased about the fact that he was the second choice. But for now, he was happy he was next on the list.

"Let's get going," Nitya said revving the engine.

~

They'd been riding for close to an hour. It was the nth time riding pillion with Nitya but her riding ability hadn't yet ceased to amaze Rishi. Though there was a shorter route, Nitya had mentioned that she'd be taking the more familiar route via Bangalore to reach Tumkur. A longer ride simply meant more fun in Nitya's books.

 However, it was the detour that caught Rishi off-guard.

He'd heard about the famed '*Sholay Hills*' often. The conversation during a typical journey from Bangalore to Mandya, especially when undertaken by road, would invariably bring up the mention of the film *Sholay*, an iconic motion picture of the seventies. The film buff that Rishi was, he remembered telling Nitya in passing how he rued never having visited Ramanagaram, the location where the film had been shot. He had also shared a rather silly desire of his.

Now, he was there, standing atop the very rocks where arguably the most famous sequence in the history of Indian cinema had been shot.

Rishi unbuckled his belt in preparation. He was about to deliver a performance that millions of kids belonging to his generation had delivered to guests in their living rooms. Not him. He was standing at the exact spot where Gabbar Singh had!

"Hmmm… Kitne aadmi they?" Rishi walked up the rocks dragging his belt.

"Sardar…. Do they" Nitya joined in.

"Hmmm… Do aadmi…

SOOWAR KE BACHCHON!!!

Vo do they aur tum teen phir bhi waapas aa gaye…khaali haath…kya samajh kar aaye they?

Sardar bahot khus hoga sabasi dega kyoon?

DHIKKAR HAI…"

The two of them burst into laughter, laughing till they almost cried.

~

"Good performance there Rishi. Still prefer Amjad Khan though. You simply aren't menacing enough. You are just too cute to be Gabbar Singh."

"You know what guys are thinking when a girl says you are cute. Don't you?!"

Rishi looked up sipping his filter coffee. They'd stopped for breakfast at one of the highway side *Thatte-Idli*[15] joints that Bidadi was famous for.

"Yeah well! But I am not like the other girls...I..."

"The reason I like you so much," Rishi said involuntarily even before Nitya had finished.

It was Nitya's turn to look up. There was no reaction on her face. None at least that Rishi could read. He thought of explaining himself. He let the thought pass.

A while passed. Rishi continued pecking at his Idli as Nitya drifted into her thought.

"You didn't get to finish what you were saying," Rishi said taking the jacket Nitya was handing out.

"I would have ruined it."

The silence though uncomfortable had probably done its job.

____

[15] A form of Idli or the South Indian rice cake, the size of a quarter plate, popular in parts of Karnataka.

XVI

They entered the campus of Siddaganga Institute of Technology (SIT) at the outskirts of Tumkur with just enough time to register for the written elimination round of the quiz. They finished on top of the pile.

It was past noon. There was a one-hour break before the final round started. Nitya and Rishi decided to grab a quick lunch. The SIT canteen was right across the street from the auditorium which was to be the venue for the quiz finals. Given the fact that it was lunchtime and an intercollegiate festival was underway, the canteen was jam-packed.

The buzz in the canteen though had nothing to do with the ongoing cultural festival. Oblivious to the same Rishi went and ordered a *Thali*[16] for Nitya and himself.

"We could have got two more questions right but not bad for a makeshift *jodi*[17] eh?"

Rishi nodded his head, his attention divided between waiting for the man at the counter to announce their token number and wondering why everyone had gathered around the television set in the far corner.

"You seem lost. What's on your mind?" Nitya queried. Rishi could sense the mild irritation in Nitya's tone for him having not echoed her enthusiasm.

---

[16] Indian equivalent of a fixed menu platter, preferred usually for its convenience and or economy.
[17] Couple

"Nothing! I was just wondering what the commotion over there was about. Never mind," Rishi said dismissing the thought. He heard the man call out their token number.

As he walked back to the table, he heard the chatter near the TV set build up. He did not allow curiosity to get better of him and walked straight back to the table where they were seated. They finished their meal quickly and headed back to the auditorium.

~

They had just finished the penultimate round of the quiz. After six rounds of quizzing, they were third and trailing the leaders by a sizeable fifty-point margin.

Rishi and Nitya simply were not in the zone! Rishi blamed himself. A couple of direct questions were sitters that he should have answered in the normal course. There was something amiss. Something about the incident in the canteen kept on bothering him. His sixth sense was telling him something. He just couldn't figure out what.

"Come on!" Nitya gave him a hard jab while the quizmaster explained the next and final round. "We haven't reached this far just to give it all up! Focus!!"

Nitya's jab served as an electric jolt that revived Rishi who was flat-lining in terms of the quiz. He trained his attention to the quizmaster.

"It is a winner take all jackpot final round with two hundred and fifty points at stake. Twenty questions on the buzzer, the answer of each serving as a clue to the final answer or the theme. Each correct answer will fetch you ten points and take you a step closer to the final answer.

Minus ten for a wrong answer. You can answer on the pass. We go clockwise. If no one gets it right, too bad!

After we have crossed ten questions, teams can buy clues for the un-answered questions, again for ten points. The answer though is revealed to all the teams!

Any team can call for the jackpot at any stage during the twenty questions and take the two hundred fifty points at stake by cracking the theme. The downside; you get it wrong and you are out of the quiz.

Good luck! May the best team win! "

~

"Pssst... I think I know what the theme is," Rishi whispered into Nitya's ear.

He had been jotting all the answers down. Thus far, seven of the nine questions had been answered. Rishi and Nitya had got two answers right, one directly and one on the pass. So had the leading team. They had now inched to second place courtesy of a couple of wrong answers by the team that was second at the beginning of the jackpot round.

He tapped on the notepad in front of him drawing Nitya's attention to what he had scribbled. He wanted to be discreet, any display of excitement on his part could alert the other teams.

Nitya glanced at what Rishi had on the notepad. Shining through all that was scribbled on the notepad were words written in capital letters. He had encircled them and as Nitya looked on Rishi underlined each one of them.

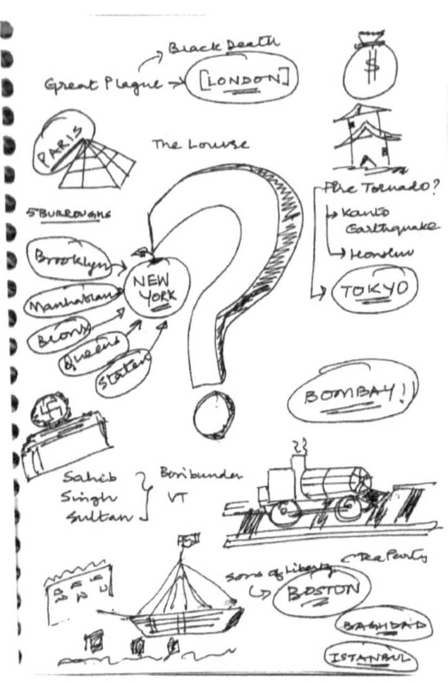

They were the names of different cities! On his notepad
Rishi had London bracketed next to the words Great Plague
and Black Death, Paris with The Louvre, Bombay next to
a sketch of what Nitya presumed were railway tracks. The
names Manhattan, Bronx, Staten, Queens, and Brooklyn were
encircled with an arrow pointing to New York, then there was
Tokyo with the words Fire Tornado written above it. She could
also see Istanbul and Baghdad written on the edges of what
was a page full up to the brim!

Rather cryptic, if not read in the context of the quiz that was
taking place. Quizzing is an innate talent. You do not become
good at it by reading guidebooks or Mastermind editions. Yes,
reading in general helps but what really matters in a quiz is the
ability to quickly retrieve random information tucked away

in a remote corner of your brain. Quizzing is mostly about "getting it"!

Nitya's face lit up as she whispered, "Let's wait for just one more question. Then it'll be ten."

"Wait! The theme! It's not that obvious!" Rishi hissed, urgency writ large on his face.

Barely had he finished his sentence they heard the buzzer. It was the team from Bidar. Rishi's heart sank!

"We'll go for the jackpot." The girl from GNDCE said confidently.

"OK!" the quizmaster said not letting go of the opportunity for histrionics.

He kept the tension alive as he recounted the team standings. MIT, Manipal was in the front of the pack, Rishi and Nitya were second but the gap was a wide fifty points. The rest of them were bunched together. The team from GNDCE, Bidar was sixty points behind with the home team SIT, Tumkur, and RVCE, Bangalore rounding off the tail seventy and eighty points behind respectively.

"Team Bidar, we have eleven more questions to go in this jackpot round. Thus far, we have seven questions that have been answered and two that have gone unanswered. You are currently third with sixty points to your credit."

Oh! Get on with it!!

The quizmaster was revelling in the moment. This perhaps was the drama he had hoped would unfold while he was designing the round. One of the teams falling prey to the lure of winning, betting on their instinct! It's not if, it always is a question of when! He continued his script by recounting each of the seven questions that had been answered and the two that had not been.

"So, Team Bidar! What's the thread that binds? Your answer will decide the fate of this contest. Glory or gore, how will your story end?!"

All that was missing was a drum-roll.

"Cities of the world!" the girls from Team Bidar answered in unison.

The quizmaster didn't react to the answer. At least not immediately. His hand on his chin he said almost wondering aloud, "What about them?"

It was Team Bidar's turn to ponder. Nitya was getting fidgety too. Rishi held her hand, giving her a reassuring squeeze.

"Two hundred and fifty points and a win at stake, after ninety minutes of quizzing, do you really think this is the answer that merits a jackpot? Team Bidar you have ten seconds to build on your answer."

Team Bidar was too shocked to recover from the blow the quizmaster had dealt.

After what seemed like the longest ten seconds in history the quizmaster ruled, "We now have four teams in fray. Goodbye Team Bidar!"

"The tenth question," he continued in a business-like tone, devoid of all the drama that had been present barely five minutes ago.

"Historically known as Anfa, the present name of this port city, derived from Portuguese and Spanish translates to 'White House' in English. Which city am I talking about?"

No sooner had the quizmaster finished, Rishi went for the buzzer. For Nitya though, things were happening too fast!

"Team Mandya!"

"Going for the jackpot," Rishi pronounced. He did not look at Nitya. He had an inkling earlier, now he was sure, and he was not about to risk waiting too long. He could feel Nitya's nails dig in!

"The answer to the tenth question is Casablanca and the connect is…" Rishi paused, he whispered "Happy Birthday!" into Nitya's ear, and continued, "Cities around the world whose names form a part of a motion picture title."

"Aha!" the quizmaster exclaimed, "Brave, very brave! Also, very interesting!"

The sense of theatre was back! You could tell that the quizmaster was enjoying this.

"You forget there are two questions that went unanswered. Wouldn't you rather have traded points first for the answers?"

"No," Rishi answered firmly. He could see the bewildered look on Nitya's face from the corner of his eye. "I kind of cracked them. Wouldn't have made any sense opening them up for the rest of the teams," he said confidently.

"Why don't you reveal the answers for the benefit of the audience? No negatives for getting them wrong and Team Mandya retains control of the buzzer."

"I am guessing Boston for the question on the Sons of Liberty and Nuremberg for the question on the Geneva Convention. But then, I am just retrofitting these into my theory."

"An American Werewolf in London, An American in Paris, Salaam Bombay…" the quizmaster named the movies that had the city names one by one.

"Ladies and gentlemen the winners of the Annual SIT Quiz—Team Mandya! Congratulations Nitya Ramanna and Hrishikesh Krishnamurthy!"

They hugged each other and kissed. It was instinctive!

XVII

They were sitting in a pub just off Brigade Road in Bangalore. The plan was impromptu. A plan triggered by an innocuous suggestion by Rishi that a celebration was in order. Riding to Bangalore to do so, was definitely not what he had in mind.

"Come on! We won ten thousand bucks today! One more pitcher and we can get another one free!" Nitya said, pointing to the strikes on her card.

"Can't say no to the birthday girl!"

Rishi turned around and signalled for another pitcher. The waiter manning their table disappeared into the kitchen. The music stopped, the waiters gathered behind Nitya's chair and one of them tapped her on the shoulder.

"Happy Birthday to you
Happy Birthday to you
Happy Birthday dear Nitya
Happy Birthday to you

From good friends and true
From old friends and new
May good luck go with you
And happiness too…"

Pecos pub was singing the birthday song as they rolled in the cake.

XVIII

It was not a very long walk, a kilometre give or take. Riding back to Mandya did not make any sense and they both agreed. Nitya wasn't comfortable leaving her bike parked at the pub, but she had conceded on Rishi's insistence.

They had to leave the pub in a hurry. Word had spread that the situation in the city had turned tense. The rumour was that mobs were setting vehicles alight. The pubs were pulling their shutters down. People emptied onto the streets.

There fortunately was no panic. Ironically, there seemed to be sobriety in the inebriation!

~

"This way Mrs. Krishnamurthy," the bellboy pointed towards the elevator. He had insisted on carrying their haversacks up to their room. They had checked themselves in at the St. Marks Hotel which was located a few blocks away from the pub they were at.

"Some cheek!" Nitya whispered tugging at Rishi's sleeve. "You actually signed us in as husband and wife?"

"Would I have dared? It's the couch for me either way," Rishi said as they entered the room.

The bellboy left disappointed. Neither Rishi nor Nitya had

paid heed to his expectant smile after he had placed their bags near the cupboard.

~

Nitya returned after a quick shower to find Rishi's eyes glued to the news. Rishi pointed to the television screen.

As they absorbed the visuals that were playing out on TV, the enormity and the gravity of the happenings of the day that they had been so blissfully oblivious of, dawned upon them!

"They razed it to the ground!" Rishi said in disbelief. He turned off the news in disgust.

"Do you think we are safe here?"

"Guess so," Rishi said giving Nitya a squeeze. "Actually, I have no idea where things go from here."

Nitya looked up and leaned in. They found themselves locked in a kiss! Gentle and tentative at first, their tongues intertwined as the intensity grew. It was a kiss that had been a long time in the waiting. There were signs that this could happen. Their subconscious acts of affection had been giving them out all along.

It is strange how love manages to squeeze itself into situations and make space for itself. Especially, around other equally strong emotions—fear for example.

There was no time for thought or even preparation as they fell onto the bed. Rishi ran his hand through Nitya's hair, still damp from the shower. Her hands had somehow managed to slip under Rishi's shirt and he could feel her fingernails digging in.

"Wait."

She took off the T-shirt she was wearing and wiggled out of the track pants. His clothes were off almost on cue. There were glances that were stolen but no words were spoken.

They got back to the kiss. The warmth of their naked bodies fanning the passion. Nitya rolled on top of Rishi. They moved to a rhythm, kissing each other, caressing, building it up to a crescendo. Their bodies seemed to know each other well. Very well!

XIX

The morning of December 7th brought realisation along with it. What followed in the aftermath of the events of December 6, 1992, altered the course of Rishi and Nitya's lives. Also, of Indian history!

Rishi woke up a few minutes earlier. The rays of the morning sun had managed to slide through the drawn curtains and were falling on Nitya's face giving her an angelic glow. She was cuddled up next to him. Still in his arms, still naked. He could see the contours of her body through the sheet. Flashes of the night gone by danced in front of his eyes. He was beaming, he was happy.

Sure he had a crush on her. He had also hoped that he would someday be the subject of her amorous intentions. But, this, a night of lovemaking had not even crossed his mind.

There were of course factors to be considered – DJ for instance.

Nitya stirred. Rishi quickly tossed between wishing her an over-enthusiastic good morning that avoided any reference to the night before or a peck on Nitya's forehead.

"Oh boy! We are in big trouble. Aren't we?" Nitya said planting a kiss on Rishi's chest as she rolled into his embrace. Rishi went with the peck on the forehead!

"I just think we are in love!" Rishi tightened his embrace.

Nitya looked up. They kissed. They made love again.

~

It was past noon by the time they finally got out of bed. Nitya ordered in the brunch while Rishi freshened up.

The newspaper was still in the cloth bag next to the food tray. Rishi pulled it out.

'Outrage in Ayodhya: Babri Masjid Destroyed.'[18] The headline screamed. The entire front page had been dedicated to the reportage. The editorial had made its way there too. Rishi read it out loud.

"…..what is vital is to recognise that this is a defining moment in India's history, a moment at which the country can be plunged into a dark abyss of primitive emotions…."[19]

The telephone rang interrupting the flow. Nitya answered. Rishi remained lost in the newspaper.

"It was the front office, I had asked them to prepare for check-out," Nitya paused, there was distress in her tone. "The army is staging a flag march in nearby Commercial Street and Shivaji Nagar. Things have taken a turn for the worse. Some incidents have been reported around Mysore too. They are advising the guests to stay put and not to venture out. At least, for another night. There's a police picket right outside the hotel and they say it's safer here."

"Hmmm… but we just have…"

---

[18] From The Hindu, December 7, 1992.
[19] Excerpt taken from 'Unforgivable' the editorial published in The Hindu, December 7,1992.

"I asked them. They'll not be charging for the room. Just the food," Nitya said.

Rishi walked across and hugged her. "People would be worried, let's make a few calls and let them know we are okay."

~

They checked out the morning after next. They lived out the two days and nights like mayflies, as though there were no more. Each moment drawing them closer, yet taking them further apart.

XX

Melange kept Rishi busy. The days and months that followed involved a lot of preparation for the intercollegiate festival. Drawing up the list of events. Deciding on the venues and timings. Avoiding clashes between marquee events. Sending out invitations to other colleges. All this, in between regular and the additional lectures that were taking place to make up for the time lost.

The college had remained shut for over two weeks owing to the communal tensions that had flared after the Ayodhya incident.

Most students went home, as did Rishi and Nitya. When they came back things got exactly the way they weren't supposed to be between them—awkward!

He couldn't have avoided Nitya totally. They were bound to run into each other. And they did!

~

It was Christmas Eve and the gang had stepped out for dinner. Everyone had decided on playing secret Santa. Each one could buy gifts for as many people as they wanted to. However, no gift could cost more than fifty rupees. Rishi picked up gifts for his roomies and Nitya. The roomies of course got a bonus. Rishi just did not want to be discovered as having given a gift only to Nitya.

Amongst the gifts that Rishi received, was an audio cassette. There was a song on the track list that had been underlined. Rishi knew!

He came back to the hostel room that night and played the song over and over again on his Walkman.

"….How do we ever keep this secret
How do we keep it in the dark…

….Why do we keep this love together
Didn't we know right from the start

That we would have to keep this secret
Or forever stay apart…"

As Rishi tossed and turned through the night listening to the song and coming to terms with the fact that the dream had ended even before it had begun, he had an epiphany.

How can I possibly lose something that was never mine, to begin with? We had an awesome time together! Three beautiful nights that shall remain etched for a lifetime. That's just how much you get and you know that's way more than what you gave yourself Rishi old chap!

As resolute as he was, he knew it was going to be tough tiding the few months that remained before Nitya graduated.

This too shall pass!

Melange helped and in a big way.

XXI

Rishi and Satya were catapulted into protagonist roles for organising the intercollegiate festival. They were like generals marshalling troops. When they spoke people listened. When they issued instructions, they were followed. H.I.T was witnessing a hitherto unimagined change in the way things worked.

Terms like senior and junior didn't seem to exist.

Change of course does not go down well with everyone. There were several folks across batches who were not too happy. Especially the growing popularity of 'Those English speaking boys' from the first year. They had a name for them too!

~

Trouble perhaps had been brewing for a while but it came to a boil on the first day of Melange. The night of the first day to be precise.

It had been a roller coaster of a day. From a point early in the morning where the organising committee was wondering if any colleges would turn up at all to a whopping twenty-five colleges and close to two hundred participating students. To the organisers' credit, things had moved with clockwork precision and the day's scheduled events had successfully been concluded.

A rock show was slated for the evening. The college band was headlining and bands from visiting colleges had been invited to open.

The gang was together. Nutty had sneaked in three or four nips of Old Monk. The idea was to get into the 'right mood' for the rock show. They walked around to the area backstage only to find out they were not the only ones looking to get into the right mood.

A bunch of day scholars or *local-ites* as they were known, were already making merry. Some from the institute and perhaps some from the neighbourhood. One couldn't be too sure.

As they neared them, Rishi recognised one of them and knew there was going to be trouble.

~

It was Siddhu! Guru or Boss if you were a junior which practically everyone in H.I.T could have been, even a few lecturers. Siddhu was a freedom fighter! He had been struggling to get his engineering degree for over ten years now! Rumour had it that one of the lady lecturers in the Chemical Engineering Department was a batchmate and unfortunately for her, Siddhu's raison d'être.

Siddhu was in a manner of speaking, the Don Corleone of the H.I.T world. He was also someone vehemently opposed to the idea of Melange. His belief and it did have its takers, was that a cultural festival held in a college in Mandya, Karnataka should promote the local culture and language.

He was known to be affiliated to the Karnataka Rajya Raitha Sangha (KRRS), a movement fighting against

GATT[20]. Specifically, the economic impact of multi-national corporations on small farmers in the state of Karnataka.

As with any movement the fringe had its interpretation of the objective. In Siddhu's case, it was being anti-English and in stark contrast to the Gandhian principles on which the movement was founded, violence was not taboo!

"Ae Tie! Barallō illi[21]," Siddhu summoned, addressing them collectively.

Siddhu seemed to have recognised them as well. The anti-Melange brigade had started calling the Melange volunteers and members of the cultural committee 'Tie'. The reference of course was to the fact that the committee members and volunteers instead of the customary ribbon badges had chosen to go with silk neckties that had the Melange logo embroidered on them. The girls wore similar silk scarves.

Satya stubbed the cigarette he was smoking, handed the nip to Nutty, and walked towards Siddhu.

"Careful!" said one of the girls. Satya raised his hand in acknowledgement without actually looking back and continued walking.

From where they were standing Rishi could hear muffled voices at first. They were speaking in Kannada. He could see that Satya, tall that he was, had his arm on Siddhu's shoulder. His demeanour suggested aggression.

Then it started. A push turned to a shove and in an instant, they were trading blows. The boys from either side jumped

---

[20] General Agreement on Tariffs and Trade

[21] Kannada. An impolite, derogatory manner of saying come here.

into the fray. It was a slugfest till someone shouted that the cops were on their way. Blows were exchanged for a while longer. Perhaps the booze and the adrenaline had begun to dry out.

"Break it up! Now!!!" It was an authoritative shout. On cue, the fight died.

It was DJ! His arms strong enough to wedge through Satya and Siddhu and his tone firm enough for the boys to listen. Someone had run to the final year hostel and informed about the fight.

Rishi found himself standing right next to DJ with a strange concoction of gratitude and guilt overwhelming him.

"Do you want this to be the first and the last Melange?" he asked Satya and Rishi angrily.

"Guru, I had warned you not to cause any trouble during the event," he said turning to Siddhu.

"You are no longer a student of the institute and have no business being here at this hour. I'm sure Prof. Nanjundaswamy[22] will not be happy if one of his men were to have a police record."

Siddhu wiped the sweat off his brow. Still breathing heavily, his lips bloody and swollen he spat the blood from his mouth and glared at Satya and Rishi.

"*Idu antyavalla*[23]!" Siddhu threatened, warning them that this wasn't the end of it.

---

[22] President of the KRRS who led campaigns against agricultural patenting by multi-national corporations.
[23] Kannada, meaning this is not the end.

With those words, Siddhu signalled to his guys, turned, and walked away.

~

Great things they say are built with blood, sweat, and tears. Couldn't have been truer for Rishi and the boys that evening. As they joined what remained of the rock show, the band was playing *Nothing's Gonna Stop Us Now!*

XXII

Melange was a roaring success. The Tie gang was now more acceptable and the glares from Siddhu and friends had died down too. In fact, there was a truce of sorts when Rishi and Satya were invited to be a part of the organising committee of the Kannada Cultural Festival that was to be organised the following semester.

~

Relief though was short-lived as the semester-end examinations were staring at them. Studies had taken a back seat for the past few weeks. There was significant ground to cover. Room 20 was seriously burning the midnight oil.

"That's it for now, I need to sleep. I'll wake up early tomorrow and practice a little more."

Rishi had been solving problems. His opening examination was his second attempt at clearing the Basics of Electrical Engineering course. He'd had enough of Kirchhoff and his laws.

He picked his Walkman, reached out for the cassette Nitya had given him, flipped open the cover, and inserted it.

As he was putting the headphones on he heard Satya say, "*Padh le saaley! Dobara fail hona chahta hai kya?!*" He was persuading him to carry on studying lest he failed to clear the course yet again.

"Mind your fucking business Satya!" Rishi retorted, irritated by Satya's rhetorical question.

"Alright then! Go on fuck yourself further listening to that shitty cassette that girl gave you! I had warned you then and I tried doing it now. But, you obviously can't heed your well-wishers. This was the last time that I tried."

Rishi showed his middle finger to Satya.

Nutty and Oggy looked up. This was not normal. Not for Room 20 and definitely not for Rishi and Satya. Neither knew this episode meant that the two would not speak to each other for a few semesters to come. What triggered it couldn't be explained, it was one of those things!

~

Rishi did fail again.

Strangely, despite the incident, Satya and Rishi remained extremely civil in their interactions. There was no further acrimony. If and when they did end up sitting next to one another, they would even pass a cigarette back and forth!

Life continued to chug along at the campus. *Vandana,* the Kannada Cultural Festival came and went by. The team of Rishi and Satya was hailed yet again.

"For two people who have this uncanny ability to partner so well, it's annoyingly stupid of you guys to continue sulking like this," Oggy said.

It was one of those nights when the boys had stepped out of the campus for dinner. But of course! No *dhaba*[24] dinner is

---

[24] Typical Indian roadside restaurant

complete without rum!

"Ya *da…* now which one of you assholes is going to quit being one first and when?" Nutty added.

"Someday…" Satya and Rishi responded in unison. They grinned sheepishly realising they had. They clinked their glasses.

~

It wasn't as if Rishi and Satya had not introspected about the events that led to the moratorium on the conversations between them. The continued civility was a de facto acknowledgement of respect for each other's positions on either side of this battle fence that had been set up.

Rishi was aware that Satya bore his best interests at heart. It was just that his jibe that night, was one too many that a troubled Rishi could have handled. He knew that he was behind on his studies. More importantly, he was still invested in a possible relationship with Nitya. If Satya only knew that there was more to Rishi's feelings towards Nitya than a mere schoolboy crush.

Satya on his part did realise that he perhaps had stepped into an area that was too sensitive. While he continued to believe that there was no future as far as Rishi and Nitya were concerned, Satya accepted that it was Rishi's life to live.

Time would tell!

XXIII

DJ and Nitya both took up jobs in Bangalore. Nitya got a plum campus placement in an MNC. DJ took up his assignment only because it was in Bangalore. They had continued to visit the campus. Sometimes each on their own and at times together.

Nitya stayed true to her plans. Her visit to the campus would be about collecting her certificates and letters of recommendation for the universities she was applying to in the US. DJ also true to Nitya's prediction stayed devoted to only one purpose—her! He was picking either the same universities or those that were in proximity to where Nitya was applying.

~

Melange had gone on to become one of the best college festivals in Karnataka if not all of India. The alumni based in nearby Bangalore continued to participate in Melange. Some like Nitya would either host an event or judge one, while others would just come back for the party!

It was the last of the three days of the festival. The atmosphere on the campus was akin to birds leaving the nest. After all, this was the last time that the Ties were organising the event. While still a part of the Cultural Committee the participation of the founders had transitioned to being more the conceptualisers than the execution guys. The way they saw it, Melange was in safe hands.

"Here take a swig and pass," Nutty was performing his official duty yet again.

Nutty's role was clearly defined. He was the supplier of booze and boy could he tuck in a few nips on his person!

Tonight was special! There was a performance by a guest band, a six-member band rather imaginatively named "The Ties". The band members—Rishi and Nitya on lead vocals, Satya on the drums and doing back-up vocals, Jazz on the keyboard, DJ playing lead guitar, and a very reluctant Oggy faking bass guitar.

Two days of practice was all they could manage. The green room sessions were chockfull with Satya giving instructions to all and sundry. Shouting and glaring at anyone who'd make a mistake.

The dirtiest looks were reserved for Rishi who would frequently miss scale.

"Trained vocalist in Carnatic style my ass!" Satya would mutter.

Rishi had more than scale on his plate to deal with. Nitya as the female lead didn't exactly help in hitting the right note. More so, with DJ egging them on.

"You are the best partnership this college has produced! Let's see some of that chemistry!!"

A nice big swig of the rum sure revved Rishi up.

"Okay! Let's do it, guys!!"

He held Nitya's hand as they all stepped on to the stage. A

loud cheer from the crowd welcomed them. The bands that had played before them had set it up nicely. The mood was extremely upbeat. They took positions on the stage. The instrumentalists required a couple of seconds to set up.

"Alright Hri..daya… nandaaa! Y'all having a good time?" Rishi said putting on his rock and roller accent.

"All the girls say yeah… and the boys," Nitya checked her mic.

"Yeah…" the crowd echoed.

DJ strummed the opening of *The Look* by Roxette as the crowd roared louder recognising the song.

"One, two, three, four, walking like a man

Hitting like hammer…"

They performed four more numbers. The high of *The Look* was followed by *Purani Jeans* by Ali Haider - a veritable college anthem, and the mellow of a not so popular Bollywood song from a movie called *Purana Mandir* but an absolute H.I.T favourite–*Woh Beetey Din*. They then built back the tempo with the freshly contemporised Gompie version of the Smokie classic - *Living Next Door to Alice*. The crowd was more than happy to join in.

"Alice? Who the fuck is Alice".

It was 1996 and no college rock concert during those days was considered complete without the popular Eagles number *Hotel California* being performed and The Ties signed off with it!

~

"Thanks all you guys, this is the best send-off ever!" Nitya said.

They'd gathered in the green room.

"Wait. What?!" DJ could not believe what he'd just heard.

So was the case with Rishi. This time, he actually paid heed to Satya's glare and his disapproving nod. He kept quiet.

XXIV

Nitya was going to the US. She was headed for Rochester University. Though over a month late she wanted to join the spring session. She also had the prospect of a job on the other side of the course. She was leaving the very next weekend. A 'proper' farewell was quickly planned for Nitya in Bangalore.

The gang descended into Bangalore on the Wednesday of the following week. Nitya was flying out Friday of the same week. First to Mumbai and a day later on to New York. DJ had offered to accompany her to Mumbai but Nitya wouldn't hear of it.

All the days were planned. Basically, movies and evenings spent pub hopping. Nitya was to weave in and out of the plans based on her convenience. She needed to shop too and that wasn't something she planned on doing with the boys, not even DJ. Satya and Nutty were to offer boarding and lodging. Logistically, the perfect mid-way meeting spot, if one were to come in from Sanjay Nagar where Satya lived and Koramangala, where Nutty's residence was, would be Brigade Road. Brigade Road and MG Road formed the nerve centre of all things fun in Bangalore, anyway!

~

"That's my last drink for the night boys," Nitya said.

They were sitting in a quaint little restaurant just off Brigade

Road—Uncle's Pub.

"Oh! Come on! Just one more!" the gang said in chorus.

"I so wish! I am afraid I have already had one too many. I promised my parents I'd have dinner with them. Do not want to walk in sloshed!"

"I'll drop you," DJ said finishing his drink.

Rishi thought he'd caught the dilemma in Nitya's eyes. He avoided looking directly at her lest his emotions betrayed him. The three years that had passed since, had abated his feelings for her. But, much as he had tried, time had not completely doused the flame. It was a moment filled with extreme pain.

It's over. It has been for a long time. Get a grip!

~

"Hey! I have an idea!" Rishi said. As DJ and Nitya rode away.

Satya and Nutty gave Rishi the look that said, "What in heaven's name has he come up with now?" However, it was Oggy who actually said it.

"Great weather for a ride. Let's go to Nandi Hills. It shall be super fun guys! What say?"

"Yeah! We can load up on beer on the highway. Maybe even carry some with us. We can hang around till the sun comes up," said one of the others.

"Great! A night out! We can head straight to the airport," Rishi chirped.

Satya wasn't pleased. Rishi could see him having a rather animated discussion with Oggy and Nutty.

The rest of the gang was in favour. The thought of a mid-night bike ride and beer for a bunch of engineering students was like preaching to the choir.

Dismissing Satya's protests, the group set off for Nandi Hills on their bikes and scooters.

"*Tera bhai Kinetic chalayega*," Rishi said to Nutty as he took the rider seat of the Kinetic Honda suggesting he wanted to ride the scooter.

"*Saala!* A couple of drinks and the *Dilliwala*[25] in you comes alive eh?" Nutty said.

They were at the foot of the hill. Rishi had been riding pillion with Nutty. Oggy was with Satya and there were two other bikes.

"The fucker doesn't know how to ride a bike. He will not be able to ride on this *ghat*[26] section… say no!" Satya told Nutty.

"Nothing will happen *da*. We barely have a kilometre to the top. Let him."

Rishi under normal circumstances, would not have gone ahead with his silly suggestion. Now that he'd heard Satya, he did!

They started off leaving behind Satya and Oggy to wait for the rest of the gang to catch-up. The assumption was, that Rishi being a novice, would ride slow enough for everyone to reach the top of the hill at the same time.

Rishi negotiated the first couple of bends well. Nutty was liberal with his words of encouragement.

---

[25] Colloquial reference to a resident of Delhi.
[26] A term that refers to the winding roads on hills. Typical to the sub-continent.

"Nothing to it *machan*."

Emboldened, Rishi gave an extra rev to the accelerator as he negotiated another bend. He was riding close to the banking. The Kinetic Honda hit a bump and wobbled. Rishi, inexperienced as he was, could not balance the scooter. In what seemed to be a flash he lay sprawled on his back, the scooter fell over to the other side, and Nutty, miraculously, was left standing!

"Oh shit! Oh shit!" Rishi could hear Nutty cursing. He expectantly waited for his roommate of four years to lend him a hand and pick him up.

To his dismay and surprise, Nutty's attention and sympathy had immediately gone to the Kinetic Honda. The rear-view mirror was broken, so was the indicator and the front fender had a dent.

"My mom is going to kill me *da*..." Nutty mumbled on.

Rishi somehow managed to stand up and dragged himself to the parapet of the culvert. When he wiped his brow, he realised that he had a deep gash that was bleeding. He felt a strange sensation enveloping him as he found his body breaking into a sweat. He ripped open his already torn shirt and pulled down his jeans and lay down on the parapet.

Meanwhile, Nutty turned his attention away from the dented scooter to his roomie only to find him sprawled almost naked on the roadside. His concern if there was any, manifested itself in a sinister kookaburra like laugh—an uncontrolled one at that.

"You okay *da*?" Nutty asked still laughing. He reached for a cigarette, lit it, and handed it to Rishi.

"Here, this might help suppress the adrenaline." He blew out the smoke as he did.

The rest of the gang came around the bend to the vision of a half-naked Rishi sprawled on the parapet and Nutty bent over him blowing smoke. The Kinetic Honda lay *in situ*.

"I knew it! I warned you this bugger will not be able to negotiate these bends." Satya fumed as he quickly parked his bike to the side of the road and ran towards them. Some others saw the humour in the picture they had just been presented with.

Oggy took a look at Rishi's gash.

"This will need some stitching up," he pronounced his verdict.

"Someone, hand me a beer," Rishi who had somewhat recovered in this time said sitting up.

"Nothing doing!" Satya said. He was clearly concerned about Rishi's injury.

"You and I are riding back to the first hospital or nursing home that we can find!"

~

They did exactly that. Rishi found it prudent to listen to Satya this time.

"It seemed like a scene out of Hindi movies…" Satya said over his shoulder. "If I did not know better, I'd have sworn that you just had been raped. With you lying naked and Nutty blowing a whiff. Classic!"

They both laughed heartily. It had been a while. Then again, it didn't seem like it. At all!

XXV

Tears rolled down his cheeks. DJ wiped them away but much as he tried, he couldn't prevent more from rolling down. He was hurting… bad!

"Woh jaa rahi hai yaar…" DJ kept repeating the words 'She's leaving man!' almost like a chant. Rishi could feel a lump in his throat too. Yet, here he was offering his shoulder for DJ to cry on.

Of all the people in the world!

They were about seven of them not including Nitya's parents and sister. Good for them, they had decided to buy tickets to the visitors lounge at the HAL Airport. The lounge was relatively empty. Nitya finished checking-in her baggage and made her way back to the perimeter separating the lounge from the passenger area. The guard did not bother stopping her.

This was it! It was time for goodbye.

Nitya was giving and getting the customary goodbye hug. As she approached DJ, one could see that her eyes were moist too.

They stood facing each other. DJ trying to delay the inevitable. Nitya moved in and planted a kiss on DJ's cheek. He kissed her forehead and hugged her tight. Unable to say a word.

"Try not to miss me," Nitya said to DJ as she broke the embrace.

It was Rishi's turn to bid goodbye. He hugged her. The only physical contact between them after that eventful night that they'd shared. She planted a kiss on Rishi's cheek too.

"What we had together was something special," Nitya said, "I'll never forget that. Never!"

She moved on to her sister and then finally her parents. Nitya sought their blessings by touching their feet.

As she turned to walk away, she waved to everyone one final time.

~

Rishi hugged DJ before they dispersed.

"Woh chali gayi yaar! Chali gayi!" DJ lamented about the fact that Nitya had left.

 Rishi felt a strange concoction of relief, guilt, and heartache. As though something had come to an end. Or had it?

DELHI

~

Four Years Later

XXVI

A bhishek Mishra and Vikram Bhatnagar were Rishi's closest friends. They were from the same school and also from the same locality in Delhi. They had been thick as thieves for as long as Rishi could remember. Life had taken them to different geographies after school, but the distances had not altered their bond.

Appearances of course had changed since their days at school. Vikram had maintained his tall and lanky self, while Abhi, over the years, had moved from being athletic to rotund.

~

"Why the hell did you opt for Bombay?" Abhi said in an accusatory tone.

"It is Mumbai now," Vikram corrected Abhi.

Abhi glared at Vikram and threw one of the cushions at him, "Like I care!"

They were at Vikram's house. Bhattu as friends would usually call him had quit an undergraduate program in the United States of America midway and joined the family business. Since his return, Bhattu had been instrumental in reviving an ailing garment manufacturing business and turning it around to become a market leader.

Abhi, on the other hand, after his graduation, had set up a small-time security agency. He now had a decent client base and a steady albeit modest flow of income.

Just to underline the fact that he now was an independent adult, Bhattu had chosen to refurbish the *barsati*[27] and had moved to the floor above. He had turned it into the quintessential bachelor pad equipped with a kick-ass projection system hooked to a stereo, a minibar and most importantly, separate access! Beer in the evening while watching a game or listening to their favourite music was a post-work ritual for the boys. Tonight was special, Rishi was leaving town.

Rishi after completing his engineering had very briefly and unsuccessfully flirted with entrepreneurship. The aborted romance was promptly followed by a couple of low paying *"Not gonna take me anywhere!"* job stints as well. Again, very brief!   Rishi had then decided to further his employment prospects and enrolled himself in an MBA program. This time, against everyone's belief he did complete the program and with flying colours.

Rishi, during the program, had interned at one of the advertising agencies in Bombay. Despite bitter experiences in the local trains Rishi had grown to like the city. Not that he would have admitted as much to his die-hard *Dilliwala* mates.

Rishi had been lucky enough to get placed in an organisation of his liking. Having finished his initial management trainee stints in different departments and at various locations across the country, he had now been in Delhi for a while. A little over eighteen months give or take.

---

[27] A small rooftop room. Usually a one-room apartment on the terrace with a veranda outside.

Rishi had just announced that he was switching roles and his new place of work would be Bombay or as it was now known, Mumbai.

"I did not really ask for Mumbai. Just that the role I am interested in is not available at Delhi," Rishi said responding to Abhi.

"I think you are just running away," Abhi said refusing to back down. He knew Rishi only too well.

"Running away?! From what?"

"You tell me Rishi. All I know is I can't be too far away from the truth."

"Calm down guys. Let bygones be," Bhattu stepped in to diffuse the tension that was brewing.

"The fact is we are here, together and it may be a while before we meet again," he paused, raised his glass, and said, "Through thick and thin!"

Rishi and Abhi echoed, "Through thick and thin!"

XXVII

He liked her. They had only been out on a date four times. Notwithstanding the fact, there was an endearing quality about her that attracted Rishi. She was petite, had short hair that finished just above the nape of her neck. Come to think of it, Rishi knew little else about her save the fact that she was pursuing a degree in English from Delhi University and that she was from Mussoorie.

Rhea Bahadur was not your typical small-town girl though. Her confidence belied the size of her hometown and her small stature, else she would not have been a single girl hitchhiking in the big bad city of Delhi. If that was not enough, she'd even accepted a ride in a car with three boys in it!

Rishi, Bhattu, and Abhi were driving through Greater Kailash towards Defence Colony in Delhi. It was Bhattu who had first spotted her — an attractive girl hitching a ride.

~

"*Baba*[28] would kill me if he ever found out!"

"Not on every occasion would you find a knight in a sweatshirt and jeans in the back-seat of a car."

"Make that three knights" Rhea quipped back, "Still not very sure you are 'The one'!"

---

[28] An affectionate reference to one's father. Popular in some parts of erstwhile Northern UP or Uttarakhand.

They burst out laughing.

Rhea had brought her friends along. Rishi, however, could see that this, "My friends meet your friends," experiment was not really going the way Rhea had hoped.

Abhi did not want to bother himself with any conversation let alone prospects of a relationship with the opposite sex.

Bhattu on the other hand was getting cold vibes from the girl he was interested in. It was often the case with him. In general, the girls Bhattu would like tended not to reciprocate the feeling. Tonight though, it did not matter! Bhattu did not need to rely on his charm to work. Time would do the trick! The girls had no real chance of ignoring him completely. It was a Saturday night and they were all going dancing.

~

Rishi since his return from Mandya, had decided to set up his own IT hardware business. Businesses that started out from garages seemed to be doing rather well those days. Rishi would assemble PCs and set up computer networks for small businesses. The first few orders had come in from friends, family, and acquaintances. The business wasn't exactly rollicking but the way Rishi saw it, was enough to keep Appa and Amma at bay. They were not exactly the business types and were keen for Rishi to pursue higher studies and get a 'proper' job.

The beginnings of his business were humble. Supported by capital from his father Rishi had assembled three computers for Bhattu's factory. Word of mouth had led to a few more orders. Primarily, from Bhattu's vendors and clients. Abhi who was running his security service agency would on his part scout for opportunities to position Rishi in his accounts. Rishi had been successful in converting the few leads that he had got into successes.

With the money he had made thus far, Rishi had been able to return the amount Mr. Krishnamurthy had invested. He had also managed to set up a small office in the commercial complex in the neighbourhood and even had two diploma engineers working part-time with him. Towards the end, Rishi was making enough money to cover his costs and even leave a little to spare for his indulgences. Then, one day, after one of his inexplicable bouts of introspection, Rishi figured that he would not be able to create the next Apple Inc. and decided to wind the business up.

He then took up employment one after the other at two small-time IT organisations in Delhi. With one, as a Sales Engineer, and with another as a Software Engineer. The organisations, however, failed to meet the high standards of Hrishikesh Krishnamurthy.

It was then that Rishi decided to equip himself with a management degree.

~

Rishi would spend most evenings with Abhi and Bhattu. The schedule had remained unchanged through Rishi's entrepreneurial stint, his fleeting employments before the MBA program, and more recently, his job. They would go to the bowling alley or play snooker or just sit around listening to music over a beer at Bhattu's or catch a movie.

It was one such evening while Rishi was in his final semester of the MBA program that Rishi met Rhea.

XXVIII

"What was she like to be with? Come on! You can tell me," Rhea asked Rishi. They were talking about exes and crushes. Rhea had never dated anyone before. Rishi opened up about his feelings for Nitya.

Rishi smiled. "We never really dated. I don't think you could even call it being in love. She wasn't in love with me then. I think I am pretty sure about that now. We had some good times together and that's all that I'd like to remember."

"Her loss entirely," Rhea said as she squeezed Rishi's hand and planted a kiss on his arm.

She just about reached his shoulder and would often not bother trying to reach his cheeks or lips. She would just plant a kiss on his arm or chest or wherever was more convenient!

~

In the year just gone by their relationship had changed gears quickly. Rhea would practically spend all her time with Rishi.

Bhattu had mastered the art of signing Rhea's hostel out-passes every weekend. A fifty rupee bribe in the hostel office had ensured his telephone number and address were on record as that of the local guardian.

They'd not spoken about it but there seemed to be a tacit acceptance that this was something more than just the usual dating routine. Abhi too had warmed up to Rhea and would often tease her by calling her *Bhabhi ji*[29].

Rishi would often sneak Rhea into the house on nights that they partied late. It was a wonder how they'd not been caught. Amma, observant as she was, had either not found conclusive proof or had chosen not to confront Rishi about Rhea spending the nights with him.

The nights that Rhea didn't sneak in were spent at Bhattu's. On the morning after, Bhattu would definitely make it a point to mention to the two that he'd slept like a log. The wink and a thumbs-up gesture to Rishi would appear the instant Rhea wasn't looking his way.

As they say, nothing lasts forever!

Amma was still up when they walked in. There she was, standing near the refrigerator with a bottle of water in her hand. It was past two in the morning.

There was only a fraction of a moment available for either of the three to react. Someone had to say something and Rhea did.

"Amma..err..Aunty...I..." she said hesitantly. Rishi looked at her, praying some intelligent excuse would come out of her mouth to explain her presence in their house at that hour.

"I've got my chums earlier than I expected and I desperately needed a sanitary pad."

Rhea did not need to finish her sentence. Amma disappeared into her bedroom and came back with a pack.

---

[29] Sister-in-law. Typically used in North India in the context of brother's wife.

"Here," she said, her voice was laden with the affection only a mother could shower.

Rishi's relief, however, was short-lived.

"*Nee vaa…*" she called him as she turned towards him and said, "I want to have a word with you."

Rhea stepped into the bathroom on cue.

"How often have you been bringing her home?"

She did not wait for Rishi to respond. He could not.

"I know!" she said as emphatically as she could without raising her voice.

Rhea stepped out.

"You both are adults and I'm not going to question your actions. You must however remember that there are consequences to your actions," Amma moved her attention to Rhea. The next few minutes went by with Rhea punctuating Amma's monologue with "Yes Aunty" and "No Aunty".

Given the context and circumstances, heading out again at that hour was not an option. They obviously couldn't have both retired to Rishi's room either! Rishi had to take the couch in the living room.

~

By the time he was awake the senior Krishnamurthy's and their son's girlfriend were at the breakfast table. To Rishi's surprise, none of the awkwardness he had anticipated was on display. The comfort was in fact, unnerving.

"Coffee?" Rhea asked as Rishi went past the dining area.

This isn't happening!

XXIX

It wasn't for the first time that they were making love. But it surely was the first time that they didn't have to bother about anything or anyone. It was a long weekend and they had driven down to Samod, a quaint little hamlet en route to Jaipur from Delhi. A four-hour drive, give or take.

Rishi had booked one of the royal suites in the Samode Palace. Someone who had recommended the hotel knew someone who ran the place. Basically, he'd got the place for a steal! The performance incentive that he had received for the quarter gone by had, in fact, prompted the indulgence.

The suite was well appointed, a blend of the old and the modern, bedecked with antique furniture and contemporary fittings. Paintings and portraits of the Maharajas of yore adorned the walls. Right in the middle of the room was the bed with a mosquito net and curtains. There was a separate open area with a dome-like ceiling that had an intricate floral design and a skylight with a Jacuzzi underneath! A small balcony extending from the room over-looked the valley.

To describe the suite as opulent would have been an understatement! Rhea and Rishi were overwhelmed!

~

"You know I always have believed that I was a queen in a past life."

They were in the Jacuzzi gazing at the stars. The gentle breeze blowing the linen drapes back and forth. They'd ordered some wine. A much called for unwind after a long drive.

"You are!"

Rishi pulled Rhea closer and kissed her forehead. As he did, he ran his fingers gently through her wet hair. She reached for the wine glasses. Handed him one, clinked, and sipped.

Rhea rolled on top, mounting him. Her body glistened in the moonlight. Her breasts swayed as she gently rocked herself on him. Rishi held her waist helping her. He leaned forward, caressing her nipples with his lips. Rhea put her arms over Rishi's shoulders kissing him forehead first till their lips locked. Their bodies pushing against each other, finding newer heights of pleasure with each thrust. Rhea shuddered as she climaxed, almost falling limp over Rishi.

~

The long weekend did them good. They took long walks, gave new meaning to a lazy breakfast, read books out loud to each other, and made love whenever they weren't doing any of the aforementioned.

Far away from all else, they got to find each other!

XXX

It felt right! Rishi could not really think of any reason why he should not say yes. After all, it is not often that a girl goes down on one knee and asks you to marry her! Rhea was exactly that kind of girl! Spontaneous, even impetuous! She'd chosen to propose in the middle of the crazy busy Janpath. All that probably was missing was a diamond ring!

Rishi had settled in well at work and Rhea had started as a content writer at an up-and-coming news network. They had been dating for close to three years now.

"Baba and Amma are coming to Delhi next weekend," Rhea said as they sat in the coffee shop. Rishi had gone with the flow and offered her an impromptu ring he made with a cigarette foil.

"He's not well and wishes to see me married at the earliest. He's been suggesting for a while now that I meet prospects for an alliance. But, I love you Rishi. I do not want to even consider someone else. I have been putting him off saying one thing or the other till now. I could not hold him off forever. I told him about you."

"Don't think it will be too much of a surprise for Amma and Appa," Rishi responded. "They've known you a while. My mother would probably even be excited at the prospect. But…"

Relationships pass their litmus test when one can sense the

apprehension of the other. Be able to hear what has been left unsaid.

"I know you feel things are moving too fast," Rhea said holding Rishi's hands.

"It's not like we are getting married tomorrow! The day after might be a possibility though," she said breaking into a laugh.

"Meet the parents it is," Rishi joined in.

~

And so, the parents met. Sure enough, there was the awkwardness of a *Tambrahm*[30] family meeting a *Kumauni*[31] family. A strange lack of understanding of each other's traditions and protocols to be followed prevailed. It was not really a formal engagement. That is, no rings were exchanged. It was more like the parents agreeing to agree.

Whatever it was, worked just fine for both Rhea and Rishi. No more questioning glances from Mrs. Vaidehi Krishnamurthy or the pressure to get married from Mr. Maan Singh Bahadur. Their respective spouses, Mr. Janardhanan Krishnamurthy and Mrs. Ratna Bahadur were just happy that there was one less thing that their partners would crib about.

While the couple now had the blessings of the two sets of parents, the same could not be said about Abhi and Bhattu.

The two of them, more so Abhi believed that Rishi was jumping into marriage a bit too soon. Abhi's objection was not about the "Why her?" it was about the "Why the hurry?"

---

[30] Colloquial reference to Tamil Brahmins
[31] People hailing from the Kumaon region in India.

Bhattu concurred. The boys felt their friend hadn't spent enough time with Rhea. At least, not enough to decide that she was the one he should get married to.

Friendship much like love, can read between the lines, hear the unsaid and at times voice it too!

XXXI

"Can't afford to rest on your laurels Rishi. Not yet at least. We need another big win if we are to meet our quotas for the year. A hundred percent gets you by, a hundred and fifty and we're talking about a direct entry into the President's Club."

~

It's rare for a boss to be liked, loved, or for that matter even respected by his subordinates. Prasanna, Rishi's boss, didn't belong to that breed of bosses either. In fact, Rishi was pretty sure Prasanna didn't want to! What he did want, was to win and he rode the boys hard for that.

"Winning comes at a cost," Prasanna would often be heard saying. "Any cost!!"

Prasanna was a graduate from one of the Ivy Leagues. Columbia, Rishi reckoned. He'd started his career with Perfect Business Machines (PBM) in the United States. He was reportedly one of the fastest rising stars in the PBM galaxy worldwide. Prasanna had moved to India a couple of years ago to join International Computers Incorporated (ICI) and was one of the four regional business heads in India. Again, the youngest member of the Leadership Team of ICI India.

Success had indeed come at a cost for Prasanna. A personal and a professional cost. He had sought to move to India despite promising prospects in the United States. As good as he was from a professional perspective, the personal downside was that Prasanna had turned an alcoholic. Rumour had it that his wife had abandoned him. Because of his alcoholism, she apparently had returned to India while she still was pregnant.

Nobody seemed to know for sure or know anything more. Prasanna was intensely private and given his aggressive nature, no one wanted to pry either!

The conversation that he and Prasanna were having, was about a new set of accounts that Rishi was being assigned.

"The tender is due to be floated in about three months," Prasanna was updating Rishi about one of the accounts.

"If we nurture this relationship and do our job well, we'll have a significant advantage over the competition. Spec it right and we'll win the biggest ever IT hardware and services contract in the history of ICI. Fifty thousand PC machines along with accessories, consumables, and maintenance! Just imagine the revenues that we'll rack up!"

Rishi couldn't help thinking how sinister the glint in Prasanna's eyes was. Rishi nevertheless, was careful even with his thoughts. He did not want to get into the wrong side of Prasanna's books.

"Go meet them as often as you can. Feed them with our product specifications, comparisons with our competitors, place demonstration units. Leave no stone unturned. Blend in, become one of them. Wine and dine them if you have to."

"There will be expectations," Prasanna continued. "We will have to figure out ways and means to fulfil them."

~

Rishi got down to business in earnest. Over the next couple of months, he had mapped the accounts well. He knew exactly who the influencers were and also, how they could be influenced!

XXXII

The Office of the Director General of Information Technology or DGIT as it was referred to, was the decision-making body concerning the hardware and software that was to be used across government offices. Each year, on behalf of various government departments, tenders worth thousands of crores of rupees would be prepared, floated, and finalised by this body for procurement of IT hardware and software.

The directorate was a four-storeyed building nestled amongst others in the Administrative Offices Complex or the AOC as it was known. Getting inside the complex itself, let alone the DGIT was a challenge.

Not so for Rishi. He knew most of the Central Industrial Security Force (CISF) guards manning the gates and entry points. There were barely one or two with whom he hadn't engaged in a conversation. Borrowing matchsticks, offering a cigarette were ways Rishi would employ to start a conversation. He made it a point to read their names on the breastplates and more importantly, remember them! Once acquainted, he would greet them with their names calling their attention whenever he would visit. If he didn't find them at their usual stations, Rishi would enquire about their well-being or when they were due to be back on the roster from the guards who were posted in their place. Yet another of his ways to start a conversation.

Rishi could if he so desired enter and exit the DGIT premises without the mandatory gate pass, asset check, and signatures.

It's amazing how far a smile and a personalised greeting can take you!

Rishi was eager to prove to Prasanna and the bosses above that he was worthy of his star performer badge. He had worked closely with the officers in the directorate on every aspect of the tender that was about to be floated. In a post-liberalisation India that was just beginning its IT transformation journey, a procurement of over fifty thousand computer machines, accessories, and software at one go was a mega event. At least a dozen companies were vying for this deal and perhaps five of them were worthy of it too.

The process of tendering is an enigmatic one. Bound to be. For the real mystery, or one may say the art, lies in fixing the ultimate winner of the process without any participant feeling left out or betrayed. Fair play rules—albeit virtually. At all times any specifications listed out should in their range, ensure the inclusion of a minimum of three qualifying vendors. That said if one were to list out all the specifications and use them as filters, at best one or two would make the cut. The trick lies in playing on the number, order, and significance of the deviations from the requirements. The real art is in making it seem as if there is no perfect vendor! In short, fix the process without it seeming fixed!

Rishi had set his sights on becoming a part of the Product Management team at ICI. The position would take him to Mumbai initially and eventually as Rishi saw it, places! The job with ICI and Rishi excelling at it, would in large measure be a vindication of the flip-flop choices he had made right after his engineering.

Being asked to work on this account had come as a blessing

in disguise for him. The level, detailing and product understanding that was required to work on this tender was unbelievable. In building the specifications he had interacted with the Product Management team in the country and participated in conference calls with the global teams as well. This account and Rishi's work were getting a lot of attention in ICI.

Despite a reluctant start on this account Rishi had started enjoying the work he was doing. Moreover, he was super pleased with the tender document he had ghostwritten. He had given ICI an 'in' on the account. A better than fighting chance!

He had done his bit. It was showtime!

The Director General had asked Rishi to arrange a meeting with the top brass of ICI. This was supposed to be a special meeting on the sidelines of the pre-bid arranged with top brands.

This was Rishi's opportunity to showcase his understanding of and the relationship built with this account. His ticket to getting what he wanted.

~

The Director General's chamber was the size of one of ICI's branch offices! There were no pretensions regarding the power and authority that the position wielded. The large mahogany table behind which the Director General was seated was the centrepiece. The table itself was three quarters the width of the room. Four chairs faced the Director General's chair. There were two more seating areas just as you entered the room. One, a round-table with four office chairs, placed on the left as one entered the room. The other on the right was a sofa set arrangement. One single-seater with a high back at the head of the coffee table and a two-two-two seater arrangement on the other sides of the table. Again, leaving no room for any doubt regarding where the Director General would sit.

The room itself, was panelled floor to ceiling with enough bookshelves to put a school library to shame. Of course, there were all the signature trappings of a government office. The portraits of Mahatma Gandhi and the Prime Minister adorned the wall right behind the Director's chair. A tabletop flag had its pride of place on the mahogany desk. Rishi was certain that tucked under the huge desk, was also a standard government-issued footrest!

The Director General got up from his chair and walked halfway across the room to greet the four-member ICI team. As he did, he gave a soft signal to the usher who disappeared closing the door behind him.

Rishi introduced the ICI team. Present for the meeting along with Prasanna were the Business Head of the Asia Pacific region, Stephen Smith, and the Chief Marketing Officer of ICI India, Ramprasad Sharma. Prasanna had made sure the top brass were there for the meeting. After all, he had an axe of his own to grind!

On the DGIT side, other than the Director General, were the two officers along with whom Rishi had worked on the tender document.

The Director General sat down on the single-seater sofa and requested the delegation to take their seats.

"I must compliment you on your selection," the Director General said in his booming voice.

"This boy Rishi is a very diligent worker. He has helped the directorate immensely. Our understanding of the product has improved manifold because of his efforts."

The two officers nodded their heads in agreement.

Rishi had expected a mention, not such profuse praise. He was blushing. Well, almost.

The Director General then went on to explain the significance of the procurement, how futuristic the outlook of the current dispensation was, and how he and his department were driving the vision of an IT-enabled India. A well-rehearsed and perhaps even an overused pitch. The two officers did their bit by continuing to nod their heads in agreement.

Steve and Ram took turns complimenting the Director General and reinforced ICI's commitment to India and India's impending IT revolution. Steve made sure to mention the fact that ICI had recently made a multi-million dollar investment in setting up a manufacturing plant for computer systems near Chennai.

It was almost like a mating ritual. The sexed-up male trying to win over the fertile female!

The meeting lasted forty-five minutes and in the end, it was just one gesticulation of the Director General that the ICI team could leave with.

"We know ICI shall take care of all the requirements, but as you are well aware, this is going to be a tendering process. May the best proposal win!" the Director General said holding up his hand with the index and middle fingers raised and parted like a 'V'.

A victory sign Steve thought it meant. Ram, Prasanna, and even Rishi knew different!

~

Ethics and integrity are pretty lofty words. Often used in professional circles, but rarely demonstrated. Rishi knew it was time to take a back seat. He had done his job! He knew that from here on Prasanna and his 'Win at any cost!' theory was going to take over.

XXXIII

They were meeting after a while. Between Rhea and work, Rishi had found little time to spend with Abhi and Bhattu. It was boys' night! A much-needed respite for Rishi from the recent overdose of Prasanna.

They were out playing snooker. It was a cosy parlour in the neighbourhood. A favourite because it was accommodating. The owner of the joint would let the boys play on late into the night or early into the morning depending on which way you looked at it. Once the shutters were down, they could pull out the beer they'd often leave to chill in the refrigerator. The owner would give company for a round or two and post that the boys could stay on as long as they wanted to. They just needed to down the shutters and leave the place clean for the next business day!

~

"Point two percent is peanuts!" Bhattu said as he just managed to break the snooker that Abhi had set up for him.

"*Aadha taka to chalta hai,*" he said in a matter-of-fact businessman tone, indicating half a percent was par.

Rishi had just brought his friends up to speed with the happenings in his professional life and shared his predicament.

"I think he's striking the same deal with anyone willing. At least with all the big players," Abhi said potting a red.

"I wouldn't be surprised. It's a deal worth almost three hundred crores. There's no way they'll award the entire contract to one vendor. Most probably, they'll split it sixty-forty in favour of the lowest bidder. Give out forty percent to the other vendors that match the price," Rishi supplemented the discussion.

"In fact," Rishi continued, "I have forecast only thirty percent of the deal volumes to my factory over the next six months. Prasanna isn't really happy about that bit though. He believes we can swing the entire deal!"

"Well, my dear Bud Fox! Your Gordon Gekko is saying greed is good. I for one, don't disagree with him!" Bhattu said alluding to the popular movie, *Wall Street*.

"You know what I think," Abhi said as he cleaned up the black and wrapped the game, "If you do crack this deal, your friends on the inside won't really mind sending a part of the *moolah*[32] your way."

 "You guys don't think I would do something like that. Do you?!"

What had just been said scared the shit out of Rishi. If his best friends could think that this was a possibility, what was to prevent the ICI management from thinking the same?

"Don't you go over analysing things now," Bhattu said sensing Rishi's angst.

---

[32] Informal, colloquial term for money.

"Dude! The fact of the matter is, whether you take a cut or not, you are involved!"

~

Abhi's words kept ringing in Rishi's ears for many nights that followed. He could see his Product Management dreams vanishing into thin air. He needed to find a way out this mess.

XXXIV

Rishi must have done something right after all. Having spent an entire morning avoiding a discussion with Prasanna regarding the DGIT tender, the call from Ram was a very welcome development. Ram had asked Rishi to join the rest of the Product Management team for a Chiptel Seminar on Next-Generation Processors. While the seminar was scheduled for two days, Ram had asked Rishi to plan the entire week in Mumbai. Also, if he did not mind, the weekend!

~

He barely had time to change into a fresh set of clothes. He entered the seminar hall late and towards the end of the first session. A delayed flight while coming in from Delhi to Mumbai had not helped his plan. Rishi had actually intended to reach the evening before the event. Prasanna however, had sulked for a few days before approving Rishi's travel requisition and his tickets just couldn't be booked on time. As it is, flight tickets were above Rishi's pay grade and the travel had been made possible by Ram's approval as an exception. Here he was now, walking in late to find the only vacant seat right next to Ram! Rishi offered a hasty greeting to Ram, picked up the seminar folder placed on the seat, and sat down.

The speaker of the first session had just wound up and the Master of Ceremonies began introducing the next speaker.

"She does India proud at the Chiptel Headquarters," the

emcee announced, "A computer engineering graduate from Mysore and a doctorate from Rochester, she has four patents to her credit and an equal number more in the offing. Having worked at the cutting edge of innovation, she has now chosen to dedicate her time to evangelising the use of Personal Computers in the field of education. Please welcome our next speaker, Dr. Nitya Ramanna!"

Rishi's jaw dropped.

~

He'd wondered about it often. About where and when their paths would cross if at all they would. Now that they had, Rishi had to admit that it was at a point in his life where he'd stopped wondering.

There she was, her short hair pulled back into a pony. If you could call it one that is. A hundred clips were holding her hair in place. Yet somehow, there was a wisp that had managed to escape. Rishi could almost count her down to the second as she'd pause to blow the wisp away from her eye.

Despite his rapt attention, Rishi had barely assimilated a word of Nitya's speech. It brought back memories of the first time he had seen her. When the house lights came on for the Q&A, he found himself desperately ducking behind other people's heads. He could see Ram looking at him expectantly from the corner of his eye but putting a question to Nitya was the last thing on his mind.

Or perhaps, he had way too many questions bubbling in his head to ask just one!

XXXV

"Avoiding me are you?" she whispered into his ears as she picked up a dinner plate. "Someone had mentioned that you were with ICI. Didn't quite expect to see you here though. I was told you were in sales."

"On the contrary," Rishi said. "I was just checking if you indeed could manage a Q&A session without help." He winked.

"Are you staying here? Can we catch up after the sessions today? Maybe…" Nitya continued tentatively. "You know… there are things that need to be said…"

Rishi nodded his head in confirmation. They exchanged numbers.

~

Rishi knew it would be difficult interacting as much and as freely with Nitya as he wanted to. He was there only for a few days and his schedule was packed. He needed to spend time with the Product Management team and of course, Ram. He was to spend the remaining part of the week with the team. Professionally , it was important he did. This probably was his one chance for making the transition to Product Management that he so desired.

On the other hand, it was Nitya whom he'd not seen or spoken to since… forever!

He needed to find the time. Fortunately, there was an opportunity at hand. Two nights! He was staying at the Lands End for the duration of the seminar and then he was due to move to a hotel closer to the ICI office in Mumbai.

Cocktails and dinner were scheduled for the evening. Rishi was strangely both excited and nervous about the evening that lay ahead.

"I hope you have some sort of dinner jacket or suit. The programme for the evening of the first day is a formal event," Ram had reminded him over the phone. "Not exactly a black-tie event though."

Rishi didn't have a clue as to what exactly black-tie events were and what needed to be worn. He had borrowed a nice black jacket from Bhattu before leaving for Mumbai. He hoped to make do with it. As he slipped the jacket on over his crisp white shirt, he checked himself in the full-length mirror next to the door.

Dapper!

~

She was wearing a long black gown with a square neck, the pearl choker added to the subtlety. Nitya had worn her hair loose. The nerdy clipped hair look had given way to a stunningly elegant one! Rishi just hoped he could keep his eyes off her.

One of the team members had already enquired whether he knew her well.

"We graduated from the same college. She was my senior." He had brushed the question away.

Nitya moved around the hall interacting with different groups. Rishi stayed on with Ram and the ICI team. However, his mind was elsewhere. It took a while before she circled to where Rishi and the ICI team was sitting. She exchanged pleasantries with the team. Mostly, thanking them for the compliments they offered her for the session she had conducted. From Rishi's perspective, they might as well have been for the way she looked that night!

Having had a few drinks and nibbled at the snacks Ram was the first to excuse himself.

"We'll let our hair loose over the weekend boys and girls, we have an early start again tomorrow," Ram said. "Mr. Krishnamurthy is the lucky one! He doesn't have anywhere to drive to. He can afford another drink."

Over the next half-hour or so, the others left too.

He was finally alone. He looked around the room for Nitya. She was standing with the Country Head of Chiptel, engrossed in conversation. Their eyes locked for a fleeting second.

Minutes later, she joined him at the bar counter.

"Let's step out."

XXXVI

Castella da Aguada or the Bandra Fort, as it is popularly known, is a short walk from the Lands End. They had made their way to the fort wall that overlooked the sea. They didn't speak much. In fact, not at all as they had walked.

"This is something that I have so longed to enjoy again...." she took a deep breath and continued, "a comfortable silence I mean."

The gentle sea breeze wafted through her hair and from where Rishi stood the gibbous moon gave Nitya a halo. She clasped his hand tight.

"I..." there was hesitation in her voice, "... don't know where to begin Rishi. I am afraid that it's gonna come out all wrong..." she trailed off. They were still holding hands. Rishi gave hers a reassuring squeeze.

"I am all ears and we have all night," he said. "In fact, two!"

There were was so much he too wanted to say. Rishi held himself back. Something told him that Nitya had been waiting for his patient ear for a long time.

~

"I have made a lot of mistakes in the years that have gone by Rishi. I have ended up hurting a lot of people. God knows I have hurt you. And… if it makes any difference, I never meant to. Of all the things that I've ever done, walking away from you was the hardest," she looked into his eyes searching for forgiveness in them.

"There was a lot that I wanted to achieve," she continued, "I was convinced that the only way to do that was to rid myself of anything or anyone that'd hold me back. I had made myself believe that DJ wasn't good enough for me because he didn't have a plan for himself. He wasn't ambitious. Or so I thought."

The serenity of the waves hitting the rocks was broken by the shrill sound of a whistle. Somewhere in the distance, Rishi could hear someone, perhaps a police constable shouting instructions, asking people to leave.

"Then you came along…" Nitya continued unperturbed.

Before Nitya could complete what she was saying the police constable intruded. The whistle blew again, this time louder and closer.

"Chala… chala… ghari ja!"

Rishi tried to steal a few minutes from the cop but in vain. The police constable moved on to the group of boys who seemed to be hanging around just for the sake of a dare. Rishi looked around and realised that he and Nitya were practically the last ones remaining.

"Chala… utha… ghari ja… naytar aatamadhye takikla ekekla!" the constable shouted in Marathi threatening to lock the boys up if they didn't comply and leave immediately.

"Think we better go," Rishi took Nitya's arm. She seemed lost. Oblivious to all the surrounding commotion.

The night was far from over!

XXXVII

Thank God for coffee shops and bottomless cups! By the time Nitya and Rishi walked in, the office dinner was over. Even the last of the drunks had left. They walked into the coffee shop. It was empty save for the hotel staff.

The coffee shop overlooked the sea and if one peered hard through the thick glass, they could make out the silhouette of the fort too. Basically, a similar view to what they had sitting at the Bandra Fort. The only difference, the sound of crashing waves replaced with piped western classical music. Nitya did not want to order anything. Rishi ordered coffee for himself.

~

"I knew you had a crush on me. DJ had figured it out too. What I did not realise, was my own attraction to you. Here I was, thinking that I was all sorted. DJ was not going to be in my future. Then, I went right on and fell for you! I tried not to though. Hard! Real hard! And… and you were so young… God damn it!" she heaved a sigh of exasperation.

Rishi could see she was distant. Perhaps reliving the past as she spoke. Thinking, taking her time to perhaps say what she had to, and the way she wanted to. He finished his coffee and signalled for a refill.

"When the admission finally came through, I was extremely happy. I had spent a couple of years working, though DJ was always around we weren't dating, more importantly, I had successfully distanced myself from you. The way I saw it, you too had managed to put 'Us' in the past," she gesticulated the air quotes and involuntarily as she normally would, blew away the stray strand of hair falling over her eyes.

"Rochester kept me busy. I signed up for an integrated Ph.D. program. My research kept me occupied. I was writing and presenting papers at every available forum. I started working for Chiptel while I was still doing my research. I was living my dream!"

She stretched her arm across the table. Rishi held her hand.

"Sunny and I met for the first time at a seminar. I'd walked across to congratulate him for the brilliant presentation he'd made. I must admit, I was the one flirting. We had a few drinks later on and a few more drinks later, I was in his room!"

She squeezed Rishi's hand before letting it go slowly, her fingers lingering on his.

"A year later, both of us were in New York working. Sunny with PBM and I with Chiptel. Our offices were located in the World Trade Centre. We would meet up often and we got along fabulously. It wasn't long before I moved into his apartment.

He was good looking, he was ambitious, and his career graph was on the uptrend! All the things in life that I, at that point in time, had wanted for myself and was working towards! We seemed like a perfect match for each other."

She reached across, picked his cup up, took a sip, and placed it back.

"He proposed. I was turning twenty-eight, he was thirty. It just felt like the right time to get married. We did!" she sighed again.

Nitya was staring into nothingness. She remained quiet, sobbing. Wiping the tears that had started to roll down her cheeks. After some time she stopped trying to fight them. She seemed to have reached a dark phase of her life.

"The abuse didn't start till after three or four months. I had seen him drink and drink copious amounts of alcohol. I never had really seen him lose control or become violent. I still remember the first time..." A shiver ran through her.

There was a lot that was pent up inside Nitya. Rishi understood, felt glad even, that he was her release. It was time for another refill.

~

"I'd returned late from work that evening. Sunny was home and he clearly had been drinking for a while. I don't really know why he'd started drinking or why he had so much to drink. He asked why I was late. I remember telling him that there were some visitors over at our office and we had a late evening meeting followed by dinner. I just reminded him that I'd called him a couple of times earlier during the day and that when he did not respond I sent him texts informing him of my plans. He snapped and smashed the glass to the floor. 'Don't lie to me, you did no such thing!' he said. I told him I wasn't fucking making it up. Before I knew it he'd closed in on me and he had me pinned against the wall his arm across my throat almost choking me. I'd never seen or experienced such rage. I somehow got the words I am sorry out of me and he let me go.

I went to the next room and closed the door behind me. I think he continued drinking through the night.

When I woke up, he was sitting at the kitchen counter with a cup of coffee. He'd prepared breakfast for me. He apologised for his behaviour and swore he'd never do it again. He told me he was taking the day off from work to sleep it off. Frankly, I was too shaken and afraid as to what he'd do if I didn't accept his apology. So, I nodded an okay and left for work.

I realised there was no one I could share the happenings of the previous night with. I sulked for a few days and he kept on trying to make it up to me, bringing home flowers, buying gifts for me, and fixing dinners. He was on his best behaviour. I caved thinking it was one of those one bad night kind of things."

~

It was dawn. They returned to their rooms.

Nitya was due to take another session post-noon, so she had some time to rest. Rishi though needed to get through the full day of the seminar. He showered, shaved, and returned for breakfast.

He had enough coffee in him to keep him awake for a week!

XXXVIII

He wasn't really sure whether it was the coffee that helped him get through the day or the desire to spend more time with Nitya. They'd spoken briefly during the lunch break where Nitya had told him that she was extending her stay.

~

"So?" she said.

The seminar had closed at five-thirty in the evening a little beyond the five o'clock close as per the agenda circulated. Much as he'd tried to hasten his return to his room, it was six-thirty by the time Rishi said his goodbyes to the rest of the ICI team and some other delegates.

He took a quick shower. Just as he had slipped into his T-shirt and jeans he heard a knock on his door.

"Up for more coffee?" Nitya had not lost time either!

"Just coffee?" Rishi said checking with Nitya, "We could head into town…"

"Or…" Nitya said stopping him short, "Check at the reception desk for things to do in Bandra!"

They did and there were indeed a few options in the vicinity. Nevertheless, once the concierge mentioned the basilica Rishi knew where they were headed.

Armed with directions they set off on their short ten-minute trek to Mount Mary Basilica.

"Always wanted to light a candle at the oratory," Nitya said as they walked.

"Just can't believe I didn't think of it earlier."

~

The lights outside were coming on as they entered the compound giving the imposing basilica a warm glow. The main entrance to the basilica had towers on either side. Each rose majestically over a hundred-feet high ending with a cross mounted over their octagonal steeples.

As they stepped into the nave, the crowd inside was thinning. They walked up to the altar. Nitya took a step forward. Rishi remained standing where he was, watching Nitya as she got transported.

She knelt, her eyes closed and hands folded in prayer. She got up and walked up to one of the pulpits.

"Come along," she whispered as she took Rishi's hand.

He followed her as she climbed up the stairs and quietly took a place beside her. Nitya once again stood in prayer. This was a side of Nitya that Rishi had never seen. He could see the calm descend on her face as she prayed.

Next, Rishi and Nitya came out of the basilica, walked across the road to the stalls and bought some candles. They climbed up the steps of the oratory opposite the basilica still holding hands. They lit a bunch of candles each and placed them in front of the statue of Mary. The light from the burning wax gave the marble an ethereal radiance.

As they walked down the steps Rishi could see that the visit to the basilica had done Nitya a world of good.

"You know what?" Nitya said, "I could sit here all day!"

"Why don't we then?" Rishi said. "There's a café not far from here, we can pick up a shake or coffee and come back here. There's more to this place!"

They walked down to the Café on Bandstand. Rishi picked up a cold coffee. Nitya wanted hers with ice cream. They took the table by the seaside.

~

Just like the waves that were rhythmically crashing on to the rocks below, memories started flooding Nitya.

"Sunny had been avoiding alcohol. He even joined AA[33]. I quit too just to make sure he stayed on course and felt that he had my support. Sobriety had taken us back to being a happy couple again. Soon, I discovered that I was pregnant!"

Nitya had been toying with her cold coffee and ice cream. Rishi broke his eye contact with Nitya and threw a glance at her glass coaxing her to eat before the ice cream melted away.

"I was a week into my second trimester when Sunny returned home late one night. He had slipped. When I confronted him he was apologetic. He said it had been a tough day at work and he just could not resist the urge! He swore he just had a drink this one time and that he would never do it again. He even admitted to it in his AA meeting."

---

[33] Alcoholics Anonymous – A global non-profit organisation that helps alcoholics attain sobriety and stay sober.

She took a look at Rishi who had finished his coffee and asked him, "More coffee? Or…"

Hot or cold, Rishi reckoned he was done with coffee. He shook his head indicating a no. Nitya too abandoned the strange-looking concoction that her cold coffee with ice cream had turned into.

They started walking towards the basilica again.

"I always had this lurking feeling that things could go downhill and quickly. But I kept telling myself to think positively" Nitya said, as she slid her arm through Rishi's.

They walked for a while in silence. It was a longer walk this time. They needed to get to the other side via the rear exit. The eastern side of the basilica and its steps were famous for the annual Bandra fair and its myriad interesting stalls that lined both sides. It was quieter around this time of the year.

"I think I ignored all the signs. Single-minded focus on his career, the aggression, his obsession with me, and our binge nights. They were always there you know! Then again. One actually starts to believe what they start to believe! I had managed to convince myself that this was what I had always wanted. A fabulous career with great promise and a partner who was as ambitious. It was on me to keep it that way."

They went down a few steps. There was just enough light emanating from the church and the surrounding buildings for them to see the huge cross at the halfway landing. They sat down on one of the wide stone banisters that ran along the side of the steps.

"A month later, it happened again! He came back drunk again and this time he was high, very high. I didn't dare confront him. Something nevertheless had ticked him off and he kept on needling me. I kept quiet despite his provocation, waiting for the storm to pass. I attempted leaving the room. As I walked past him he yanked hard at my arm and the moment I turned, he slapped me hard across my face and yelled 'Don't you dare ignore me. You bitch!' I somehow managed to break free from his hold. I ran into the bedroom and locked myself up. He remained at the door, banging it. His rant continued through the night."

Rishi put his arm around Nitya and gave her a reassuring hug.

"The next morning when I got up, there was a strange quiet around the house. I somehow mustered the courage to open the door. I walked out to find the living room in disarray and him gone. The last thing I needed was another confrontation! I quickly packed my bags, grabbed my passport, my medical records, and literally ran out.

I checked into a hotel. I mulled calling 911 and reporting the incident but decided against it. His stock in PBM was on the up during those days. For all that our relationship was worth, I did not want to ruin that for him. I booked the evening flight to Pune. My parents had moved there when my father retired from the army."

I wonder…

Rishi brushed aside the thought that had crept in. He needed to be certain.

~

It was getting late.

"What say we take this conversation back to the coffee shop

like last night? We could continue over dinner and sit as late as we want," Rishi said looking at his watch.

"Or..." Nitya said building on the thought, "We could take it to my room, raid the minibar and order room-service!!!"

XXXIX

"Ibbani was born that November. It was Diwali. That evening, while the world outside was busy lighting lamps and bursting firecrackers, my little *pataki*[34] was making her way into this world!

Ibbani is Kannada for dew. Sunny and I could never agree on a boy's name. This was one name we both liked…" she trailed off.

"Sunny tried contacting me several times during the initial days. He sent me e-mails apologising for what had happened. I did not respond to him. He kept in touch with my parents and my sister throughout my pregnancy. My parents were my Rock of Gibraltar. It would have been so easy for them to push me towards a compromise, but they gave me the space I needed and stood by me.

He flew down the day after I had Ibbani. We met briefly. He told me I could take my time. I'd had a long time to think about and prepare for the inevitability of this meeting. I told him that I did not plan on going back or getting back with him. I also told him that as much as I did not deserve an abusive husband, Ibbani did deserve a father. A month later he had quit his job with PBM and joined ICI India."

What he was hearing from Nitya just then, deep down Rishi already knew! He looked up to find anticipation written large

---

[34] Firecracker in Kannada.

on Nitya's face.

"Can you hold me?"

He did and that's the way they remained all night!

XL

He was at the crossroads. Despite having returned to Delhi, Rishi's heart and mind were still there in Mumbai. The time spent in Mumbai had opened some new prospects on the professional front for Rishi and re-opened some on the personal.

Rishi knew he needed to make some choices. Hard ones!

~

"We need to make our move now or we'll lose this deal to someone else Rishi!"

Prasanna, since Rishi's return from Mumbai, had been anxious.

Normally the one to keep Prasanna abreast with the developments at DGIT, Rishi had not bothered to spend any time with Prasanna after he had come back.

Now that he knew what he knew, Rishi thought it was in the best interest of all involved that he maintained his distance. Rishi was not too sure how much, and if at all Prasanna knew about Nitya's relationship with him. Come to think of it, Prasanna did know which engineering college Rishi was from, but he had never brought it up in any conversation. That said, Prasanna anyway was the intensely private kind.

"Hey! You with me?" Prasanna said nudging Rishi.

"I had a word with the DG's sidekicks while you were away. We have an understanding. I also have support from Steve for making the required arrangements." Prasanna did a shadow coin flip with his thumb as he ended his sentence.

"Your good friend Ram, refused to help us out. Some principled cockamamie about not utilising marketing budget for payments that are not 'Completely overboard'."

Prasanna clearly wasn't happy with Ram. The man was taking away a resource and not even obliging to help Prasanna out with money from the marketing budget, to pay for what ostensibly was a bribe!

"I have it all worked out now. Through an alternate route of course!"

Rishi couldn't help but notice the sense of pride in Prasanna's voice.

"Steve shall arrange for the money to be paid in dollars by someone in New York to the contact there. Once the payment in New York is made, we will be notified. We can go and collect the money in Indian Rupees from their network contact here in India. It's called *hawala*[35]. The only difference, we are doing it in reverse," he said cockily.

"I am not sure if I should be a part of this anymore Prasanna. I… I mean with my impending role change and all…" Rishi said making a woeful attempt at registering his objection.

"I know," Prasanna said with a chuckle. "The truth is, neither you nor any of us have a say in this matter."

---

[35] An informal (also illegal) method of funds transfer across geographies through backchannel networks.

Rishi gave him a puzzled look.

"You are the chosen one!" Prasanna continued. "The DG, no less, says you are the only one they trust to make the drop. I wouldn't be surprised if people here at ICI begin to wonder why it's you…"

Rishi had walked right into his worst nightmare!

XLI

The intimation of handover had come the night before. Rishi had been informed by Prasanna that he was required to go and collect the money from the agent in India. Rishi was nervous, even scared. Forget cash he hadn't even seen a cheque for that kind of value his entire life! The rendezvous for the pickup was a nondescript town called Muzaffarnagar, located in the western part of Uttar Pradesh.

~

"Couldn't have done this without you guys man!" Rishi said in thankful exasperation. He was glad he had their company. There was no way he could have done it alone. He couldn't have involved anyone from work either.

Rishi had enlisted Bhattu and Abhi for the three hundred-kilometre road trip to Muzaffarnagar and back.

Abhi was at the wheel, Bhattu was sitting in front next to him. They had been driving for a while now.

~

It had taken some doing and spinning of yarn, for them to leave in the middle of the night. They were all big boys now. Nevertheless, none of the parents could have wrapped their heads around the fact that the reason for their setting out at such an unearthly hour was work! Rishi thought it was best not to mention anything about the 'transaction' that he was about to facilitate.

Mr. Krishnamurthy was a man of principles and it would have broken him if he were to find out what his son was getting involved in. Rishi so wished he'd had the courage to have refused to participate in this deal.

Rishi's parents also heard the telephone ring. Fortunately, Rishi had picked up the telephone before Appa could. It was Prasanna on the other end of the line instructing Rishi to start for Muzaffarnagar as soon as he could. He had to be there to collect the money from the agent at 9 AM sharp. He also needed to be back by evening or latest by noon the day after.

"The DG is hosting a dinner the day after tomorrow. It may well be that the drop is made on the sidelines of the dinner. We need to be ready for it!" Prasanna had said.

"Rhea's father has had a heart attack. I need to leave right away for Mussoorie!" Rishi told his parents.

No further questions were asked neither was any explanation given. Rishi gave a call to Abhi and then to Bhattu. The same story was given in each of the households.

It was past four in the morning by the time they left. They expected it to be a three and a half to four-hour drive give or take. That would get them into town by seven-thirty or eight, time enough to check into a hotel room, freshen up and get to the meeting.

Rishi felt pretty shitty for having lied to his parents. He felt worse for having made it about Rhea's dad.

~

Sona sona dil mera sona

Surme waale nain ladaake le gayi, hai!

Sona sona hai dil mera sona

"Argh! Not this song again!" Rishi cringed.

Seeing that Rishi was feeling low, Abhi and Bhattu had decided the best way to pep him up was by playing some music. The boys had got stuck on this number from one of the recent Bollywood releases and they had been playing it on loop for the better part of the two hours that they had been driving.

"Hey! I think that *theka*[36] is about to open!" Abhi pointed excitedly.

Abhi had been cribbing about the fact that he had been woken up in the middle of the night and designated driver. This was his standard operating procedure to get his beer! He'd first volunteer to drive, then crib a while later about the fact that he always had to. Bhattu and Rishi were happy to play along.

Not that morning though. Rishi was truly out of sorts. Guilt and nerves were both playing up.

"Are you out of your mind? It's 6 AM!!"

Not one to back off easily Abhi said, "Well… I am sure someone must be buying. Why else would they open shop at this time of the day?"

The logic was hard to argue against and Rishi realised that his outburst was perhaps misdirected.

---

[36] A licensed liquor vend.

"On one condition. *Sona Sona* doesn't play again," Rishi said. Bhattu snickered.

The liquor vend guy though was extremely surprised when Rishi walked up and asked for beer. He quickly went through the motions of placing the incense sticks that he'd just lit in the prayer area. From a superstitious businessman's perspective, Rishi walking in was a good omen!

Abhi was happy. So happy in fact that by the time he'd finished his first, he was back to playing the song!

XLII

They had timed the drive just right! By the time the three of them had showered and grabbed breakfast, it was eight-thirty. The hotel they had checked into was at the outskirts, not far away from the location of their meeting.

As light as Abhi and Bhattu had made of this exercise they were nervy too. After all, Rishi was supposed to receive and carry back with him twenty lakh rupees in cash! He had asked Bhattu to keep a suitcase in the trunk of the car. He figured that kind of cash would require one.

They neared a small roadside *mazaar*[37], the landmark that had been given. Abhi was at the wheel again and this time Rishi was sitting next to him. He pulled out the chit on which he had scribbled the few quick instructions that Prasanna had given him.

He was to meet a certain Anees Chaudhry. When he did, he was to share with him a transaction reference number *52H 624607* and receive a confirmation in exchange. He was to refer to Prasanna as Sunny! Finally, they were to collect the cash and drive back straight to Delhi.

"Anees Chaudhry, yahin milenge?" Rishi enquired as they drew up next to the *mazaar*.

---

[37] A Muslim shrine. Typically, a grave of a Sufi saint where people visit to seek blessings and make a wish.

"Dude! Feel as though we are part of a movie scene. Hell! This guy even has a scar on his face!" Bhattu said trying to diffuse the tension. He barely could manage a laugh himself.

One of the men gave an affirmative nod and pointed across the road.

They took a U-turn.

One actually couldn't see much of the house from the main road. The compound wall was at least nine feet high and had multi-coloured glass shards on top. A green door served the purpose of what normally would have been a gate. A traditional door chain hung on it which presumably also served as the door knock.

Rishi took it upon himself to knock while Abhi and Bhattu stood a step behind him trying to look as nonchalant as they could.

"Anees Chaudhry, yahin milenge?" Rishi enquired again, confirming whether they had reached their destination. The door had been opened by a boy in his teens. The boy immediately shut the door. Rishi could hear the boy running across the courtyard.

Rishi nervously checked the time. It was exactly nine!

The door opened in a little while. This time it was a man who seemed to be in his mid-forties. He was tall and well-built. He peered through the partially open door.

"Kya kaam hai?" he enquired about their business.

Once Rishi told him that Sunny had sent them, the man opened the door fully and allowed them in. They walked across the courtyard, not towards the house but what seemed like a barn.

There was a makeshift shed in front of the barn where a few buffaloes were tied.

Rishi wondered whether the man himself was Anees or they were being led to him. He somehow couldn't muster the courage to ask.

"Gunne ki kheti hai hamari," the man who had opened the door informed them that they were sugarcane farmers. He opened the lock of a room inside the barn. Rishi nodded his head and so did the other two. Neither was sure as to how to process the information.

They'd no option but to go with the flow.

The room itself was set up like an office. A table was placed in the centre with chairs on either side. The man pointed to the chairs asking them to take a seat as he switched on the lights and fans. Large wooden cupboards lined the wall across the table.

The three of them took their seats. The teen who had opened the door initially was back with a tray and four glasses of sherbet[38].

"Number batao," the man asked Rishi for the transaction reference. Rishi figured that the man was Anees himself. Assured, he promptly pulled out the chit on which the number was written down.

Anees opened an envelope that was on his table. Inside was a letter and a ten-rupee note. He put the letter aside and read aloud the numbers on the currency note; *5... 2... H... 6... 2... 4... 6... 0... 7!*

---

[38] A cold drink of sweetened diluted fruit juices typically served as a refreshment.

Anees handed over the currency note to Rishi as he stood up. He turned and walked a few steps and opened the cupboard that was behind him. Inside the cupboard was a large safe locker. It looked like one of those thick cast-iron ones. Anees rotated the three-armed lever in both clock-wise and anti-clockwise direction a couple of times. They could hear the locks click. He pulled the locker door open.

The locker was lined from top to bottom with stacks of currency notes! The three of them tried hard to prevent their respective jaws from dropping. Anees however was unemotional. He pulled out and placed the stacks neatly on the table. There were twenty bundles of the recently introduced thousand-rupee note.

"We probably didn't need the suitcase," Bhattu who was sitting in the middle whispered to Rishi.

The teenager was back. This time around with a large cardboard box. The way he was carrying it indicated that it was heavy.

"Tassali kar li jiye," Anees suggested, asking the boys to reassure themselves that everything was in order. He spoke over his shoulder as he locked the safe. The three boys took turns counting the notes making sure that the amount tallied.

The teen in the meantime had emptied the carton. There were jaggery bricks placed in a neat stack beside it. On cue, he began wrapping the individual currency bundles with newspaper. He then proceeded to line the carton with *bhusa*[39]. He then placed a row of jaggery bricks on it, lined with straw again, and then placed the currency notes on top. He repeated the process. In no time he had packed all the notes along with the jaggery!

---

[39] Broken straw or chaff.

Abhi picked up the carton and started walking towards the door while Rishi thanked Anees and said goodbye.

Anees instructed the teen to see the boys off.

Once outside, they placed the carton in the trunk, got into the car, and drove away as quickly as they could manage.

XLIII

They had been driving for a while now, say fifty minutes. The adrenaline had started to subside and one could tell that because the music was back at the 'are you crazy' levels. Abhi flicked out the butt of the cigarette that he was smoking.

"That was the last one. Need more smokes for the way home," he shouted over his shoulders addressing Rishi who again was in the rear seat. "A shortstop for peeing and picking up a pack. Don't worry we'll make it quick."

Rishi had reiterated Prasanna's instruction of driving straight back non-stop.

Abhi pulled into a dhaba. The boys took turns to stay in the car while the others relieved themselves.

Rishi had relaxed by now and readily yielded to Bhattu's demand for *chai.* The two of them were sipping hot tea from their *kulladh*[40] when Abhi came running. He had gone to pick up cigarettes from the roadside vend.

"Get into the car! Quick!!"

The boys didn't bother to ask why. Panic and urgency were evident.

They literally tore off leaving a cloud of dust behind.

---

[40] Traditional earthenware. A cup made of clay.

"Remember Scarface at the *mazaar*? He and another guy on a motorcycle were there at the cigarette vend. I think we are being followed."

Abhi had his foot jammed onto the accelerator pedal while Bhattu sitting in the back seat tried to look out of the rear windshield for anyone tailing. Rishi was thinking of a way out of the situation but all his mind could draw, was a blank.

Ten minutes later they still weren't sure if they were being followed. For the moment, all three concurred that it was better to be safe. The sense of relief though had turned to vapour.

Abhi had managed to maintain speed. The fact that it was nearing lunch helped. They'd been spared from the highway rush. They still had a hundred-odd kilometres to go. The boys knew they needed to cover as much ground as they could before the Sun set.

In the dark, on the highway, they were fair game!

~

Sometimes, things that happen might seem like challenges at that point in time. In hindsight though, they are godsend.

"Ab kya karein?!" Rishi despaired as they neared a police check post. The constable was signalling for their car to stop by the side for checking.

The boys looked at each other. They were carrying cash stashed in cartons of jaggery and possibly, some goons hot on their tail. The last thing they needed to add to their woes was cops checking their car! They were on the outskirts of Meerut. It surely wasn't the usual time, if not location, for a check post to be set up.

"Dilli jaa rahe ho?" said the constable who had stopped them enquiring where they were headed.

There are occasions that are tailor-made for some! Conversations with cops were Bhattu's forte! Just like an actor who's just got his cue he launched into dialogue mode.

"Ji bhai sahib! Vaise is time pe checking… sab theek to hai?" Bhattu asked nonchalantly rolling down the window as the constable peered in. The constable did not bother to respond to Bhattus's query regarding the time and purpose of the checking in progress. Instead, he went around the car, taking a good look at the boys. All of them had rolled down their windows. Abhi sensing an opportunity had lit a cigarette.

"Kahan se aa rahe ho aap log?" the constable said asking where they were coming from. For the moment, the two characters in the act were reading out of two different scripts!

Bhattu nevertheless was enjoying this.

"Muzaffarnagar gaye they bhai sahab. Humaare dost ki shaadi mein. Kal raat ki thee…" Bhattu responded weaving a tale about having attended a wedding.

Meanwhile, Rishi was back to being nervous. Abhi, true to his personality was genuinely uninterested, he was blowing smoke rings. However, Bhattu in the back seat was raring and ready with more details of this imaginary wedding that they'd attended the previous evening.

"Dikki kholo," the constable said instructing Abhi to open the trunk of the car. He did. Rishi's heart skipped a beat!

"Humaare suitcase hain aur thoda gur hai bhai sahab. Humaari bhaabi ke yahan gunne ki kheti hai," Bhattu stuck to his script and

explained the contents while two other constables inspected the trunk. *"Baaratiyon ko ek cartoon bhar ke gur diya hai!"*

They bought it!

"Dilli mein kahan rehte ho?" the constable enquired, wanting to know which part of Delhi they were from.

"Soami Nagar," Abhi said confidently blowing out smoke and stubbing the butt out. He'd stepped out to open the trunk.

"Ise Chirag Dilli chhod dena." The constable turned towards the booth and shouted, *"Mishra ji! Aa jao, inke saath nikal lo,"* calling out to one of his colleagues. The man who was to hitch a ride with them was in plain clothes and seemed to have just gotten off duty. He had a shoulder bag and was carrying his service rifle. He joined the boys in the car.

The permission neither had been sought nor was desired to be. Cops across the country pretty much believe that every citizen owes them a 'no questions asked' ride.

~

They were feeling relieved. Abhi was still at the wheel but wasn't tearing down the highway as he had been. Half-an-hour back they were fearing the worst, now they had an armed cop riding with them. They were safe. Protected!

"Aap lenge Mishra ji?" Bhattu offered the cop a cigarette and as he lit his own asked, *"Vaise ye checking?"* trying again to find out the reason for the police checks.

"Naka bandi hai…" the cop informed that barricades and check-posts had been set up. *"Kuch hamlavar Muzaffarnagar mein gangster Anees Chaudhry ka murder karke bhaage hain!"*

The boys could not believe what they'd just been told. Someone had just bumped off Anees Chaudhry!! The man they were the last to meet. Or were they? Glances were exchanged.

Scarface and the man on the motorcycle weren't chasing them. They were running away too!!

XLIV

"Shit! Shit! Shit!" Rishi exclaimed for the thousandth time. "I am in deep fucking trouble guys! Not only am I the world's biggest liar in the eyes of Rhea and my parents, I am also a murder suspect or at best a potential witness who the police are on the lookout for!"

~

If something can go wrong, it most probably will! Murphy and his law had caught up with Rishi. If it were indeed possible, his return to Delhi was more dramatic than the Muzaffarnagar episode.

It was late evening by the time Rishi finally made it back home. What followed was not pleasant!

"How's Mr. Bahadur now?" Mrs. Krishnamurthy asked as she opened the door.

As he set his bag down and walked towards his room Rishi mumbled something about Mr. Bahadur being much better, his condition not as serious as was feared, it being a long day, etc. What he was not expecting at all was seeing Rhea and Mr. Krishnamurthy seated at the dining table. Not many words were exchanged thereafter.

In fact, none at all were spoken by Rhea. She got up, her gaze slicing Rishi as she walked past him.

Mrs. Krishnamurthy picked up the car keys as she said, "It's late. I'll drop you."

In one fell swoop, Rishi's credibility and his love life had been reduced into inexistence!

XLV

The weeks that followed were tension-filled. Rishi was scouring the crime section of the newspaper every day tracking the developments on the Anees Chaudhry murder case.

Two things worried Rishi. One, the reports mentioned that Anees was still at the door after having seen off some 'guests' when he was shot at by his assailants. The second, according to them the investigation team set up by the UP Police was working on a few strong leads. The basis - a purported diary that Anees kept, to track all the *hawala* transactions.

Back at work, Prasanna had been strangely indifferent. The dinner at the Director General's residence did not take place on the day it was scheduled. There had been no word about it from Prasanna. Also, despite the news of Anees Chaudhry's murder being the hottest topic of discussion practically everywhere, Prasanna hadn't even bothered to acknowledge it. He had simply asked Rishi to instruct the office boy to transfer the carton to his car.

Disgust would have been a mild word to describe what Rishi felt for Prasanna. Prasanna it appeared, had moved on and was already thinking of Rishi's handover.

~

If something is already bad, there is every chance that it can get worse! And so it did!

"The DG has invited you to dinner, 'Diligent boy'," Prasanna said making air quotes. "The tender should be out next week on Wednesday. The handover, if the specs are as you made them will be at the dinner. They insisted on your presence. In fact, just your presence."

His tone was sinister and did nothing to hide the pure sense of joy. He seemed to have made up his mind that he wasn't going to make Rishi's transfer and transition easy.

Meanwhile, Ram had set the wheels in motion for Rishi's movement to the Product Management team and Mumbai. Prasanna however, had made Rishi's relieving contingent upon completion of the submission formalities for the tender. One way or the other, this tender was critical to Rishi's career. His work and control on the account were a subject of discussion in management meetings all the way up to the global board!

There seemed to be a new star rising on the International Computers Incorporated horizon; Prasanna did not seem to like its ascent.

~

The trail was getting hotter, at least that's what the reports said. The police had not yet been able to nab the culprits, but they had established their identity. Ravi-Munna. The two were known and much wanted criminals with a history of shoot and scoot killings. The police according to the newspaper reports, had taken a teenager who used to work with Anees into custody. The assailants had been identified with the help of the artist sketches based on the description given by the boy.

The police, the article said, believed that the teenager was vital to the ongoing investigations. They, however, did not rule out the possibility of his being complicit.

The piece also mentioned that the boy had helped the police put together the sequence of events that morning. Three men, it said, had picked up cash routed through the *hawala* network. Police had the artist impressions of these three men too. However, their faces had not matched anyone with a known criminal record. A separate case for economic offence had been registered under the Foreign Exchange Regulation Act.

~

"How long do you think before they find out that the money was for us?" Rishi said.

Prasanna was at his desk reading the newspaper.

"Not us, them!" Prasanna said as he folded the newspaper and placed it on the table. "And if luck runs out, then you... and then... us."

"Them?"

"They cannot trace it back to ICI. As far as the informal channel was concerned the payment was for a DG *Sahab* to be collected by a Sunny. Go figure..." Prasanna paused as he got up. He picked the cigarette pack and the lighter lying on his desk and started walking out of his cubicle.

"... and if they do make something from the descriptions they have, they reach you and whoever you went with and then... us. Basically, a long shot," Prasanna said cockily as he walked away.

Rishi didn't need a sign. If any of this heat were to reach Prasanna or ICI even remotely, it was Rishi who'd be hung out to dry. He was the one managing the account. It was Rishi that the Director General had praised and now invited for dinner.

Weeks away from getting his shot at a career as a Product Manager, Rishi realised the minefield that lay in front of him!

Think! You need a way out of this mess and fast!

~

A few days later, the newspapers carried a report that the Central Vigilance Commission had raided the Directorate General of Information Technology. The report said that the Directorate had been under scrutiny for a while now. However, the raid in question had been conducted on receipt of a specific complaint. The article did not carry further details of the complaint.

Inquiry proceedings under the Prevention of Corruption Act had been instituted against the Director General and his subordinates.

Consequently, all the tenders that had been floated by the DGIT during the one-year tenure of the Director General were under review and on hold, the report said.

Hallelujah!

XLVI

It was over. Rhea had made that clear. She hadn't spoken with him since the night of his return. Even Amma at home had been sending out cold vibes. Rishi had contemplated the wisdom of keeping the truth from Rhea and Amma a few times over. Nothing that he could come up with told him that the yarn that he and his friends had spun was worth its while. After all, if it was okay for Bhattu and Abhi to know, then why not his parents and Rhea?

There was another, much bigger question that had been crossing Rishi's mind though, and that perhaps was the one Rishi was searching an answer for. He had been for a while. Rishi had finally made his mind up. It was liberating!

~

Rhea, after much persuasion had finally agreed to meet him. They were sitting in a McDonalds close to Rhea's office.

"I have a submission deadline, can't spend too much time," she had said as Rishi was picking her up. A stark contrast compared to what was usual.

"I am sorry!"

Anything that Rishi had to say to Rhea needed to begin with an apology. Today more than ever.

Rishi went ahead and told Rhea about the trip to Muzaffarnagar. He did not spare any details. He told her about the situation at work that had compelled him to and all the things that transpired. He apologised again for basing the entire lie upon her father having a heart attack. Rishi emphasized that it was a spur of the moment thing. He simply had not wanted his parents, to know about his involvement with anything unethical. Especially Mr. Krishnamurthy and more so now that all the gory details had been reported.

"You know," said Rhea. She had been listening to what Rishi had to say very intently and patiently. "You started with an apology but all that followed later was just about 'You'. Not once did you express any concern or regret about what your lie made me go through."

Her eyes were moist, a moment away from a tear rolling down. She did not let it happen.

"I always knew and was even okay with the fact that I was keener. 'He'll come around,' I kept telling myself. Now, I think you just went with the flow. I am incidental in your life Rishi, if not irrelevant."

"I like you, Rhea, always have! I know that I have let you down."

"Not enough to ever put my feelings ahead of yours Rishi."

"I did not mean for it to end this way…"

"Too bad Rishi! It just has… and guess what… it's you who just ended it!"

She got up picked up her shawl and her purse and left. From where he was sitting, Rishi could see her hail an auto-rickshaw.

He could have gone after her. Maybe he should have. The fact was, he didn't.

XLVII

Relieved! Was one word that described how he was feeling. The other word was excited. Rishi now had a transfer letter in his hands. Ram had followed through on his commitment and Prasanna, albeit grudgingly, had let go.

He was with Abhi and Bhattu. They were at Bhattu's. As was the case many a time, an argument had broken between Abhi and Rishi. Bhattu had just jumped in to break it the only way he knew would work. By raising a toast!

"Through thick and thin."

There's one unmistakable quality about friendship, especially the kind that is thick; an argument is never too far or for that matter over till it is!

"Maine to tujhe tabhi kaha tha... jaldbazi mat kar..." Abhi continued his "I told you so." rant. "God knows why you were so fucking smitten!" He gulped his drink and implored the others to do the same.

"Chal na..." Bhattu stepped in again and offered the cigarette he was smoking to Abhi—the metaphorical peace pipe.

"I just think it's very convenient..." Abhi said taking the cigarette. However, he did not show much interest in attaining peace. "... running away from things is not going to solve them you know..." he mumbled as he fixed another round and handed one to Rishi.

"There is nothing to solve Abhi!" Rishi replied.

"It's something that I have wanted since my MBA days guys. The position is available and I am taking it. That's all there is to it. This would've happened regardless of all this other stuff."

"Abhi does have a point," Bhattu suddenly turned coat.

"It does seem very convenient, at least the way things are falling into place!"

"What are you talking about? Which things?" Rishi said getting a wee flustered.

"Well…" Bhattu said stopping to sip his drink.

"Oh! Come on! Don't just leave it hanging. Enlighten me." Rishi said taking a swig.

"Yes! Please do go on," Abhi joined issue.

"Okay, okay! Here's the sequence of events." Bhattu began enjoying every bit of the interest in his theory that he had generated.

"Rishi meets Nitya in Mumbai. Turns out she's married. To whom? Prasanna!! Who is Prasanna? Rishi's boss!! What does the boss do? Arguably, sets Rishi on an unethical path that makes Rishi resort to a lie. What happens because of it? Rhea breaks up with Rishi. What happens next? Rishi moves to Mumbai. Who's he gonna meet there… again… Nitya!! Convenient don't you think." Bhattu winked. His demeanour akin to a peacock strutting around displaying its plumage.

"Nah! Our friend here isn't running away. He is infact running in! To meet his destiny!"

The three of them had gravitated into a huddle.

"To love and luck!" Abhi raised a toast.

"To love and luck!"

MUMBAI

~

The City of Dreams

XLVIII

He was meeting him after a long time. They had kept in touch over phone calls and e-mails. Satya was now married. He had joined Jaya in Mumbai about a year ago. They'd tied the knot within a month of Jaya completing her MBBS.

Satya, after his MBA, had joined a popular chocolate brand and after an initial stint in Bangalore had moved to a new role at the company headquarters in Mumbai. Jaya was already in Mumbai pursuing an MS in Obstetrics & Gynaecology. The young couple had rented a cosy two-bedroom apartment in a high-rise in Khar.

"Why stay in a hotel dude? You must stay with us while you search for a place to rent."

It had been a couple of weeks since Rishi had shifted to Mumbai. The initial weekends had been spent house hunting. Rishi up until then had been unable to make his mind up and was in a quandary. Tired and frustrated, he had taken a break from his search for accommodation and was spending the weekend with Satya and Jaya instead.

"You'll find out in time that the local train is the best mode of transport. Stay as close to a local train station as you can. Don't bother about which side. No matter which direction you need to head, the trains are going to be crowded." Jaya chipped in.

Satya and Jaya were high school sweethearts. During their years of courtship, Jaya had often visited Mandya. She was more than familiar, in fact, friends in her own right with Satya's roommates.

"Also, remember to get your railway pass made. First Class preferably."

"Like Satya puts it, 'It's not that it's less crowded, it's the fact that the armpit that you are bound to be smelling shall at least have deodorant on it.'"

The three burst out laughing. It was like old times. It felt great!

~

A month turned into three and Rishi hadn't been able to find a place. Make that a place to his liking. One that was cosy and at a convenient distance from work and close to the beach and accessible and had great watering holes for taking care of the weekends.

"At the risk of getting my ass kicked by Jaya…" Satya said as he helped Rishi put the last of his suitcases into the boot and closed it, "Stop acting like a teenage girl. There is no such thing as the perfect guy!" He signalled with air quotes.

Rishi had already spent eight weeks instead of the four that were allowed as per the company policy as settling-in.

Satya's words had turned out to be prophetic. Rishi was about to stay with Satya and Jaya. He had insisted that he be considered a paying guest. Jaya had agreed and not to anyone's surprise, after a lot of persuasion.

XLIX

They were meeting for the first time since he'd moved to Mumbai. The calls too had been infrequent. It simply had not worked out that way. Between Rishi wanting to finalise a place for himself and Nitya's commitments at work and more importantly, at home, they just had not been able to make time. One thing that was sure though was the fact that both had been eagerly wanting to.

"I have missed you!" Rishi said giving her a hug.

He'd been waiting for her at the Panvel station. Nitya had taken the morning train from Pune. They took a taxi and headed straight to the hotel. Rishi had checked in earlier that morning.

"I have taken the day off so we have the entire day to ourselves."

Nitya walked across the room. She slid her arms from behind him and gave Rishi a tight hug.

"Promise me that it won't be this long before we meet again."

Rishi turned and before he could say anything they were locked in a kiss.

Their bodies had hungered for each other for close to ten years now. They'd been away from each other and with other people but as they say, the body has a memory of its own! The sense of longing overpowering enough for them to make passionate love without another word being spoken!

The lovemaking seemed to have given them their release. They fell asleep in each other's arms.

Only to wake up and make love again.

A lot of water had flowed under the bridge since the last they had been lovers. It was Rishi's turn now to take Nitya through the happenings in his life. He made sure he told her everything there was to tell. About his entrepreneurial stint post engineering, about Rhea and breaking up with her. He told her about his job at ICI and his aspirations. He told her about Prasanna, the DGIT deal right down to the happenings of the recent past.

Nitya giggled. It was evening. They were still in bed, still naked under the sheets.

"What?" Rishi nudged Nitya. His curiosity getting better of him. A mischievous giggle after all that he'd told her, wasn't the reaction that he had been expecting.

"You and I are very similar animals, victims of an odd circumstance," she said as she snuggled, "Here we are fucking each other while there's a guy out there who is busy fucking our lives! Oblivious to the fact... that we actually are fucking each other! Ironic! Don't you think?!"

"Indeed!" Rishi said as he pulled Nitya closer and kissed her.

"Also..." he said gently caressing her, "... that's more fucks in one sentence than we've got since morning! Unfair! Don't you think?!"

"I can remedy that right away..."

~

They'd stepped into a new phase in their relationship. It was the first time that they were together because they wanted to be. The first time in years that they were with each other, in a room where guilt was not!

L

"We're doing this then," Nitya said as she sipped her coffee. Rishi looked up. He had been working on his laptop preparing a presentation for an upcoming meeting.

After the initial euphoria, they'd settled down to meeting each other less frequently. There was no way Rishi or Nitya could have explained their absence every weekend either at home or at work, so they would meet on a regular workday. Nitya would take the early morning train or a bus out of Pune and the late evening bus back home. The two would then spend the day in their room in the hotel, working, talking, happy just being with each other! The hotel authorities did raise a brow initially but had eventually warmed up to the recurring nature of the business. Today was different though, it was a Friday and Nitya was staying over.

Earlier during the day, Rishi had mentioned wanting to spend time with Nitya and Ibbani in Pune. He genuinely felt that this was the next step. He believed that he needed to develop an independent relationship with the child as also with Nitya's parents before they broke the news to them.

His suggestion, as he now realised, had triggered deep thought. It was normal for the two of them to just sit around in silence doing their own thing. They were comfortable with it. He looked up. He didn't want his eagerness to prompt any decision from Nitya's end.

"Only if you are sure that it is time," Rishi replied choosing his words carefully.

He put down the screen of his laptop, got up, and walked over to where Nitya was sitting. He poured coffee from the pot that room service had just delivered.

Nitya looked up. She had tears in her eyes.

"I love you Rishi. I always thought it was a cliché to say it. Never believed that saying it even mattered. But there…" she trailed off.

Rishi sat down next to Nitya and put his arm over her shoulder and kissed Nitya's forehead.

"I love you too Nitya. I always have." He rubbed the side of her arm reassuringly. Rishi realised Nitya was not in the same space as he was, at least not yet.

"Whenever you are ready."

Nothing further was said. Nothing needed to be.

~

"Thanks a ton, buddy, I owe you this one. Big time!" Rishi jotted down the details on the notepad. He placed the telephone receiver that he had nestled between his neck and his shoulder while writing, back on the cradle.

He had just arranged for a motorcycle. A biker colleague had connected him to a bike rental near the hotel.

Nitya had come a long way from the sporty, bike riding, and the carefree girl that she once used to be. Riding was one way Rishi thought, Nitya could reconnect with her former self.

All it took was a bit of persuading. Once they got to the bike rental, Nitya was in her element. Mounting the bikes, getting a feel.

Rishi didn't know what she was looking for but was happy watching.

"This one!" Nitya told the Parsi gentleman who owned the rental. She could barely control her excitement and kept pacing around while Rishi completed the paperwork required and paid the deposit.

From the corner of his eye, he saw Nitya blowing off the stray wisp of hair. He smiled to himself.

LI

Fridays are usually the busiest day of the week at the *dargah*.[41] They were at Haji Ali. Rishi kept looking at Nitya as they walked the short length of the causeway to the *dargah*. There was an amazing sense of tranquillity that seemed to pervade the salty sea breeze.

Despite the presence of thousands of people around them and being in the middle of a crowd, they well could have been walking alone!

A tap on his shoulder served as a reminder that Jaya and Satya were just a step behind. Rishi had called ahead to let Satya know they were riding into town. Satya, always up for a bike ride, had joined them along the way with Jaya.

The most enjoyable amongst the times spent with friends are the ones with impromptu plans! The two riding enthusiasts decided to make this one count. They casually let their respective partners know that they were riding up to Matheran and spending the weekend there!

~

It was dusk. They were sitting around the campfire singing songs, sipping rum like good old days. The guesthouse had laid out the evening dinner along with an open bar counter in the lawns. The rain had fortunately stayed away and not

---

[41] The tomb or shrine of a Muslim saint.

played spoilsport.

"I am sorry I did not see it earlier," said Satya giving Rishi a nudge. The girls had gone to get a refill.

"Huh?"

"I know that I wasn't easy on you back then and kept dissuading you. Yet for some strange reason, I always believed that…" Satya paused as he picked an end of the burning wood and poked around trying to rejuvenate the bonfire.

"… she's good for you man! You guys are meant to be," Satya raised his glass.

"Thank you! Moreover, I always knew that you'd come around. You are slow that way."

The boys had a hearty laugh. As they clinked their glasses and downed their drinks, the girls walked back.

"Our turn!" The two boys said in unison and proceeded towards the bar counter. Another round was definitely called for!

~

Multiple treks to quaint spots with breath-taking views dotted the next two days.

Time was like one of the great wizards that weekend. It travelled back and forth a decade and then disappeared as easily. The trip, as unplanned and spur of the moment as it had been, had served a purpose. The four sported a contented smile on the ride back.

Not many words were spoken until they bid their goodbyes.

"I'll see you in Pune," Nitya said as she kissed Rishi one last time before she boarded the train. For the first time in years, she felt hopeful.

As the train rolled out of the station, their eyes remained locked until they could see each other no more.

LII

Recognition is great. The going had been good since he had moved into the new role. India was a focus market and Rishi's inputs on improvements, new products and the likes were being taken seriously in the ICI ecosystem. Rishi was loving the attention; even getting used to it.

Given the circumstances, the e-mail Rishi found in his inbox that morning was cause for worry. He read it many times over. It was not a very long e-mail, it was as long and as impersonal as typical system-generated e-mails tend to be. It was marked confidential – meaning that he couldn't discuss the contents with anyone. Even for clarification!

The e-mail was from the GIA team. Global Internal Audits was as the name suggested, the team responsible for conducting routine investigative audits into any business process that could be considered 'out of the ordinary'. The e-mail was to intimate the initiation of the audit process with specific regard to the DGIT deal.

As a part of the first phase, Rishi was to receive a separate, detailed questionnaire. In addition, the audit process required all pertinent files, e-mails, and documentation to be declared and voluntarily quarantined.

Once the documents had been studied by the audit team, interviews would be conducted for which a separate intimation would be sent, the mail said.

This cannot be good.

He was certain that Prasanna too would have received a similar e-mail. He thought of all the things that Prasanna possibly could, maybe even would disclose. The deal had been in a limbo ever since the vigilance raid on the DGIT and there was no way of telling what Prasanna was planning on doing next. The money had already made way to India and into Prasanna's hands. He wasn't too sure if Prasanna had passed on the money or not. Either spelt trouble!

Rishi spent a disturbed night. Regardless, he woke up resolute. He was conscious of the fact that an impropriety had indeed been committed. He was, willy-nilly, a part of it and there was nothing he could do to change that. He decided that he was going to share all the files and whatever other information that would be sought. Rishi chose to believe that he had nothing to fear or worry about. His conscience was clear.

~

It is a rather odd feeling that one gets when one thinks that everyone around them knows what one knows but, everyone does not want one to really know what they really do know! Rishi had been getting that feeling ever since the mail had hit his inbox. The frustrating part was he really could not do anything about it. So, Rishi got down to doing the one thing that he could; work harder!

Fortunately for Rishi, Ram had not betrayed any emotion in this regard. He was certain that Ram and Steve too would form a part of the audit at some point in time. That, potentially, was the point where he'd get his redemption!

Over the week that followed, Rishi meticulously pieced together the sequence of events. He literally had a timeline on paper and had jotted down the milestones. By the time the questionnaire arrived he had segregated all the communication concerning DGIT – internal and external, all the versions of the tender document he had prepared, and more importantly, verified all his meeting dates with his notes and travel claims.

He wanted to be, scratch that, needed to be, exact! This audit was bound to end with someone losing their name and position. Rishi did not plan on being that someone!

LIII

"I have filed for divorce and claimed custody in a Pune court. It's almost two years that we have been living separately." There was a marked excitement in Nitya's voice. "Also," she continued, "the fact that I have had Ibbani with me here in Pune ever since she was born should work in my favour. I fully expect Sunny to contest."

Nitya's voice at the other end of the line felt therapeutic as always. The information that she had just shared though was not what Rishi had been expecting. Nitya had always felt and Rishi agreed, that formalising her separation had to be the necessary first step before making their relationship public. However, she'd always had a 'When the time is right,' view to actually going ahead with it.

"My lawyer tells me we stand a good chance. She's warned me to be prepared for a bitter, even a long drawn battle. If I know Sunny, she's probably right about the bitter part." There was a certain sense of achievement in the tone of her voice. Rishi was glad that Nitya had finally taken the decision.

He was happy. This was a significant step forward but there still was a long way to go before the two of them could be together.

He conveyed his feelings over the phone trying hard not to sound too excited nor too pessimistic.

~

They needed to be cautious since the divorce process had been initiated.

It was clear to Rishi that his being in the picture could potentially do more harm than good for the proceedings. They needed to maintain their distance lest Prasanna or his lawyers got wind of their relationship. It would without a doubt become cannon feed.

Any hint of any relationship, let alone one involving Rishi could take the entire matter on a very different path tilting the scales the opposite way!

The process in all probability, was likely to take time, which meant that Nitya would have to keep her cool. Especially, given that Rishi wasn't going to be readily available to support her or be around her in her greatest times of need.

It was clear that this relationship was going to be tested.

He knew that deep down, Nitya had the fortitude to get through this. Just that time and circumstances had rattled her. He needed to ensure that the Nitya of the old showed up for this battle! Rishi knew the best way he could help Nitya was not necessarily by being present, it would be by being patient.

Every meeting of theirs going forward had to be carefully planned, appropriately punctuated, and yes, cautiously executed!

~

Each of them needed to fight their respective battles with Prasanna.

The road ahead was going to be a challenging one but Rishi

was sure Nitya and he were equal to it. They had won things together before!

LIV

They had not spoken since. Rhea was the last person Rishi had thought he'd be meeting. He surely had not imagined them sharing a cordial cup of coffee at a café in Mumbai!

~

"Hello!" The apprehension in the voice at the other end of the line was tangible.

"Hello, Rhea! How have you been?"

"Good… actually," Rhea said, perhaps with a pinch of remorse embedded in her voice for a relationship that had gone south. "You?"

"Same here Rhea. Mumbai has been treating me well."

"*Achha* listen…" she continued, "I am in town and was wondering if you'd like to catch up over a cup of coffee."

"Well…"

"Hey don't worry. Two friends catching up. Nothing more."

"OK no. Scratch that. I do have something that I need you to do for me," Rhea squeezed in another line even before Rishi could respond.

"Sure!"

They decided on where and when.

Rishi couldn't help wonder how the meeting was going to turn out. One really could not say that the two of them had parted ways well.

She sure sounded like she'd moved on.

All these months, somewhere deep down he had been carrying this guilt premised on having moved on so quickly. He felt relieved, however, not before a moment where he did feel bad that Rhea did not sound miserable. He chided himself for entertaining the thought.

~

"So?"

They were seated outdoors at Eat Around The Corner in Pali Hill. What Rhea had proposed as a quick breakfast and coffee before she reported at work, had turned into a longish Sunday brunch kind of affair.

Any apprehensions either of them had about meeting each other had melted away in the warm hug that they shared as they met.

In the now over two hours of conversation, they had gotten past developments in their careers and thus far managed to avoid any references to what had transpired on a personal front.

Rhea had moved up the editorial rungs within the same TV News channel and now was a part of the Business Desk. More specifically, the part that covered economic offences. The past couple of years with the match-fixing scandal rocking the cricketing world, Operation West End that had 'stung' the political world and the enactment of the FEMA[42] had created a brand new breed of investigative journalists. Rhea was one of them.

"So I'm guessing our conversation is off the record," Rishi said needling Rhea. "And that you are not wearing a wire."

"Very funny! *Vaise* I did tell you that I needed something from you."

"Name it."

"I am working on a story about the CVC raid at the Directorate General of Information Technology. I remember you telling me that the DGIT was one of your key accounts."

"Well..."

"Don't worry Rishi, I'll not name you as a source..." Rhea added sensing Rishi's discomfort.

"There's something that you should know before I tell you anything in this regard, Rhea."

~

It simply would not have been possible otherwise. For Rhea to understand anything about the DGIT or the CVC raid or the trip to Muzaffarnagar that Rishi had made along with Abhi and Bhattu, she needed to know about him and Nitya.

More importantly, Rhea needed to know about Nitya and Prasanna.

They were just about finished with lunch by the time Rishi had

---

[42] The Foreign Exchange Management Act, 1999.

gone through the entire story. Rhea had perhaps journeyed through an entire range of emotions.

From the simple curiosity of a friend to the angst of a lover betrayed. From the inquisitiveness of a journalist who had stumbled upon a whole new angle to the story to the empathy of a woman for another. Rhea experienced it all, for Rishi did not hold back a single detail.

Rishi was aware that he had hurt Rhea once before. He however was sure that regardless of how painful the truth was, it would be liberating.

It was!

LV

Rhea reached across the table and held Rishi's hand reassuringly. They'd spent the better part of the day talking. She couldn't remember a time when they had done just that. Talk. Whoever said it's overrated?!

"I'll help you fix this Rishi," Rhea said. There was unmistakable confidence in her manner.

"I have a plan. You'll need to work with me on this one."

The cheque arrived. Rishi promptly paid it. Glad that there was no niggling discomfort of 'Let's split it' or 'I'll foot it.'

"Dinner tomorrow then?" Rhea said as she climbed into the auto-rickshaw.

Rishi nodded.

~

"Are you seriously telling me this?" Satya was fuming.

It was later that evening. Rishi had seen no point in going to work that late during the day. He had decided to head back home.

They were sitting at the dinner table. Since he was home early, Rishi had decided to make dinner. He made pasta. By the time Satya and Jaya had arrived the bowl of spaghetti with meatball sauce and the wine glasses had been placed.

Rishi had mentioned meeting Rhea over dinner.

"Dude! You cannot risk spoiling this! I simply do not get this concept of 'Oh! We used to date. But now, we are just good friends!' It is a load of bull-crap and nothing else."

"Calm down Satya," Jaya stepped in well aware of the history the boys shared. "Don't go all *filmy* on him. Of course, they can meet as friends. Both of them are adults. So what if they have a past? You both have had one too. The two of you seem to have managed to put it behind alright." Jaya added perspective to the conversation.

"Rishi and Rhea hadn't exactly parted ways on great terms. This… is closure! In fact, it is good that they have something else to discuss. If the girl is saying she'll help Rishi, maybe she has thought of something. Who can say?"

"Alright, alright, I won't," Satya finished the wine in his glass, poured some more for himself and Jaya, "You better keep Nitya informed buddy," he said to Rishi as he passed the bottle to him.

"Sure!"

Rishi fully intended to tell Nitya. He just needed to know what Rhea had on her mind and be sure that her plan was tenable.

~

One can never undermine the value of bouncing things off with friends. Yes, it may at times lead to heated arguments, even heartburn, but it sure does help distil thoughts. And when done with really good friends, the well-wishers, it leads to better decisions!

Rishi spent the night thinking of all the possible ways in which he could make the help coming in from Rhea's quarter count. Whilst he did, he also thought of all the possible ways any further engagement with Rhea could jeopardise his relationship with Nitya. Unlike Satya, Rishi had no apprehensions regarding getting emotionally involved with Rhea again. He was not involved enough earlier either, his relationship with Rhea would not have ended otherwise. He was also certain that Nitya wouldn't have a problem with him meeting or working with Rhea on anything. His apprehension was a blowback to Nitya and the divorce proceedings.

One thing was clear. Here was an opportunity to get closure. For his sake and for that of Nitya's, he was going to go all out! He started typing a text to Nitya but held himself back.

Not yet!

~

It turned out to be an extremely busy day at work the next day.

Rishi found a fresh e-mail from the GIA waiting for him in his inbox. The content of the mail was a rejoinder questionnaire based on the documents and e-mails that Rishi had earmarked for quarantine.

For the moment, the questions seemed to be centred on the undue pressure the order projections and material forecasting had created on the ICI global supply chain. Significant upstream investments had gone into procuring some non-standard components that were required for complying with the technical specifications of the DGIT tender. Calls had been taken by people in the system without giving due consideration to the processes. Calls, which were way above

Rishi's paygrade!

The focus was on Rishi's role as the Key Account Manager. GIA wanted to know why and wherefrom the specifications for the products came and the process adopted for requesting the new product. Also, the underlying assumptions and logic for determining the order size and timing.

From where Rishi was seated he had a clear view of Ram's cabin. Though he had been busy drafting his response, he had not failed to notice the frenetic pace of activity across the aisle. Ram had been locked up in his cabin all morning. He seemed to be on a conference call. From the agitated manner and the way Ram was pacing around his room, Rishi reckoned it was a call that was not going too well. The Product Manager taking care of the Business Desktop product line had been in and out of Ram's cabin quite a few times.

Rishi guessed Ram would have received his audit intimation. The kind of decisions that were under scrutiny would necessarily have involved Ram. The good news was Ram had not summoned Rishi yet for clarifications of any sort. The bad news was that the shit was surely flying around now. It was only a matter of time before it hit the fan!

Stop worrying about imaginary things!

Rishi sent out his responses. Just to test his theory, he walked past Ram's cabin to get his coffee, and on his way back, he knocked on his door.

"Hi! Got a minute? Just wanted to run the rolling forecast by you. Needed your guidance on planning the transition to Montara[43]."

---

[43] Intel code name for the Intel 852 and 855 series of mobile chipsets.

Ram looked up, "Not today Rishi. The GSC and Guangdong are chewing my ass out over the projections for Vivaldi-II that we had given them." He said using an ICI code name for a line of Business Desktops and referring to the global supply chain team.

"Okay. Whenever you have the time," Rishi said trying to sound unperturbed. He closed the cabin door and walked back to his desk.

Ah! The audit guys must have reached out to the GSC. Just a matter of time!

Rishi liked Ram. He had been extremely helpful and supportive as Rishi had transitioned from being a sales guy to being a Product Manager. Ram had a very hands-off style of managing his subordinates. He was always there to guide and review, never getting in your way or your hair. A welcome relief, especially for Rishi, from the overbearing style of Prasanna. Rishi wondered whether Ram's style had possibly worked to his detriment.

That Ram could end up as damaged collateral was something Rishi had not considered.

Qué será será[44]!

---

[44] Spanish phrase meaning 'What will be, will be!' popularised by a song by Doris Day.

LVI

Rishi left work early. He initially had planned to head straight for the dinner after work hours but he could not get himself to sit. He needed some more time for thought. He did so with a walk from the Bandstand promenade to Linking Road.

Rhea and he had agreed to meet at a restaurant on Linking Road that served delectable *Kebabs* and an awesome *Dal Makhani*. Food that he knew well at a place that he knew well! The comfort of the known was an absolute essential at the moment. He was venturing into unknown territory and hinging on the success of the plan, were his love life and career aspirations; in a nutshell, his future!

~

Rhea was already seated by the time Rishi reached. She got up as she saw Rishi walk in.

"Sorry, the walk took me longer than I expected," Rishi said as he hugged Rhea.

The cordialities out of the way, they ordered themselves a drink and a *Kebab* platter.

"So…" Rhea started without losing another moment.

It was past midnight by the time the two were done with their strategizing. The bearer waiting on them had moved from politely hinting for their last orders, to asking Rishi whether he'd like to order his usual choice of dessert.

Over the course of the drinks and dinner Rhea informed Rishi that she now had a go-ahead from her management for a series of article posts. She also had made the management aware that she had a 'source' that would share information on the condition of anonymity. Needless to say, there were some rules for playing this game.

She needed to be extremely careful of any allegations that got levelled against anyone in her story and would definitely require validation. In other words, friendship and trust aside, Rishi would carry the burden of proof should at any time the story blow-up or move in an unintended direction.

Rishi however clarified that he was uncomfortable sharing any ICI confidential data. Rhea had responded to his reservation with, "We shall cross that bridge when we come to it."

"They mostly are going to be on the defensive. They are government servants under scrutiny in an ongoing government investigation. My story shall only raise the necessary amount of doubt around the CVC raid, a very large tender that was floated around the same time, the irregularities found, and a possible *hawala* connection. I'll allow the readers and whoever else to join the dots I place. Trust me."

She took a piece of the *Naan* from her plate and wiped off the remnants of the *Dal Makhani* in the bowl. Her eyes did not need to search for the bearer to fetch the finger bowl, he was waiting with it already!

"Would you like to order dessert?" the bearer asked reluctantly following the protocol.

Rhea nodded yes and continued.

"If any of the other media houses pick this story up, which one must fully expect will happen, the media pressure will exacerbate action. Basically, ICI and the other companies shall need fall guys. Small fry will not suffice, some big heads would need to roll," she paused.

"And therein lies your safety!" Rhea was beaming.

She'd have done a heel click were she not seated. They paid and made their way out of the restaurant. There was lots more to talk about and it was the weekend. Rishi hailed a taxi.

"Town," he told the taxi driver as he slid into the back seat after Rhea had.

"I am glad I mustered the courage to meet you," Rhea put her hand gently over Rishi's. "I'm sorry we parted the way we did."

"Why ever would you need courage to call me?" Rishi turned and asked her. As he spoke he slid out his hand from under Rhea's and put it on the backrest.

"Well…" she trailed off and looked out, lost in thought as though figuring out the right words to say. Rishi had tried not to make it so but Rhea surely had sensed the awkwardness.

They rode in silence until they had reached Marine Drive.

~

It was a moonless night. They had been sitting at the promenade right outside The Oberoi just watching the Back Bay waters gently hit the tetra-pods for a while. Rhea had tugged at Rishi's arm as they were getting off the taxi and indicated that she wanted to spend some time staring at the sea.

"Actually there is something else that I wanted to tell you," Rhea finally broke her silence.

Rishi turned, facing Rhea now.

"It all happened fast, you know…" despite the darkness Rishi could see tears rolling down Rhea's cheeks, "… you coming back from Muzaffarnagar, the break-up, your move to Mumbai."

"I know, I thought so too," Rishi said.

"Bhattu took it upon himself to clear your side of the story. Initially, I was still too angry to even meet him. But, he never gave up on me. Kept trying. Once I relented, he explained the entire episode and the sequence of events. It helped me put things in perspective. About you. About what happened."

"I should have tried…"

"Yes. But the fact that you did not, told me something. Something that I had been ignoring for a long time. It was then that I realised, that maybe, it was me who was keeping you chained. I never considered the possibility that it was only I who was looking for 'something more'. You, I guess, were looking for 'something else.'"

Rishi had not expected this turn of events. He had pretty much convinced himself that their relationship had indeed turned the corner and that 'this', whatever 'this' was, was platonic. Right at that moment though, he wasn't sure. He did not know which way this was headed.

"Anyway, we kept meeting after that. At times with Abhi in tow, at others, just the two of us. A movie here, a dinner there. Somewhere, over all the meeting up that happened, I developed feelings for Bhattu. Can you imagine?!" she chuckled. "At first, I held back, telling myself that I was on a rebound. But the more we met, the more we started wanting to meet. Once I was sure of myself and about my feelings, I told Bhattu. He receded into a shell, stopped meeting me altogether! Meeting you was Abhi's idea. "

Rhea turned, looked at Rishi, and held his hand, "I know Bhattu feels the same way about me. However, he will not move ahead till he knows you're okay with it. He values his friendship with you too much to even risk talking to you about it. He may never. So here I am."

Rishi felt a strange concoction of relief combined with surprise and happiness. He reached out and gave Rhea a tight reassuring hug.

"He's a great guy! I know the two of you are going to be great together. Couldn't be happier!"

They got up.

"Coffee?"

"Yes!!! Desperate for it," Rhea said, as they crossed the road.

LVII

She stirred, still in her sleep. There was a big smile on her face, an expression of calm that belied the tumult her life was in. He kissed her on the forehead. Rishi so desired waking up like this every day. He knew it would take a while but happen it would!

He got up, put the kettle on boil, and picked up the newspaper at the door. He took a quick shower. Nitya was still sleeping, curled up like a baby.

He made tea.

"Wake up sleepy head!" he said as he ran his fingers through her hair.

Nitya smiled lazily. "Why can't every morning be like this?"

"They will be… soon!"

~

They'd agreed to lay low, away from the public eye till the divorce was settled. No calls or e-mails either. They had blocked dates on their calendars the last time that they had met. The hotel room was also booked for the dates and if for whatever reason either could not make it they swore that the other would understand.

There was a lot to talk about and the two of them had done

exactly that through the night.

Nitya had filled Rishi in regarding the proceedings in the District Court. From what Nitya had told him, Rishi gathered that a lady judge was hearing the matter and thus far two hearings had been held. Prasanna himself hadn't turned up. He had been represented by his lawyer. As had been expected, the divorce plea was indeed being contested.

Nitya mentioned that Sunny's lawyer had denied any allegations of cruelty during the time of cohabitation. His lawyer had represented that the specific incident of the night preceding the day I left, was an accident for which Prasanna had apologised.

"Tch! I should have made that call to 911 that night..." she admonished her self.

"If anything, Sunny according to them was the aggrieved party in this matter. His lawyers had the audacity to claim that it was I who had deserted him causing him distress and agony! They anyway knew that they couldn't contest alcoholism which was one of the grounds of my plea. They had to cite the fact that Sunny had joined an AA help group. While they used it to show realisation and self-awareness, my lawyer says that it only strengthens our argument."

Nitya had turned wistful as she had recounted the case details.

"I don't know Rishi. Life was turning out to be just fine. I was getting used to the way it was. I was away from Sunny, I had little Ibbani who gave life a very different meaning. I even got back to work on my terms..." she said slipping further into melancholy.

She held onto the collar of Rishi's T-shirt pulling him closer almost ensuring that he hugged her tighter. He did and as he pulled her closer, he kissed her mane.

"I know it's not easy having to go through all of that torture again. This is the only way out. It is the right way out!" he kissed her again.

They were sitting on the ledge. Rishi had opened the windows and gone and sat there as he smoked. Nitya had joined him and stolen a few drags, something she'd started doing of late. From a distance they could hear the sounds of the city as it prepared to begin yet another day.

It was still dark outside, very dark. Dawn was nigh.

Rishi got up. He held his hand out to her, "Come," he said in a soft voice.

Nitya followed him to bed. As she lay with her head resting on Rishi's shoulders, she felt safe, even confident! Before long Rishi could hear her soft snores.

He pulled the blanket and tucked her. He did not miss the pale moonlight as it streamed through the window and lit the smile on Nitya's face.

~

They chose to go to the restaurant below. Nitya didn't feel like ordering in and Rishi anyway loved the breakfast spread at the hotel they were staying at. He liked the place. They seemed to like him too! The hotel management was always willing to accommodate Rishi even at short notice.

Rishi was pretty sure that he was their most loyal guest. Even without taking into account the month that he had stayed there at ICI expense, Rishi would have spent another month in room nights at the hotel over the past year. A change in the vendor at ICI meant that this hotel was off the list as far as the office was concerned. Therefore, no questioning eyes either.

From Nitya's perspective, the hotel was conveniently located. It was just off the Mumbai-Pune highway. An easy two-and-a-half-hour Volvo ride for her. Even the Panvel railway station was close by. Courteous staff, clean rooms, and good food. It ticked all the key boxes for her too!

~

"So, tell me…" she said eagerly as she settled down with her plate laden with cut fresh fruits, "How did it go with Rhea?"

It was comforting to see her excited. Nitya contrary to Rishi's apprehension had been very unemotional about him meeting Rhea. It was a different Nitya that had woken up that morning. The vulnerability of the night before had disappeared. It made Rishi understand something significant. Nitya and he were way more mature about handling each other's past relationships than he had given either of them credit for!

He brought her up to speed with the plans Rhea and he had made over multiple rounds of breakfast.

"Just be careful!" Nitya cautioned him. "I know the way these US-based firms operate. They are extremely cagey when it comes to company confidential information. Make sure you are not giving out any documents…"

She thought for a bit, staring into oblivion as she did. She pursed her lips and blew the errant wisp off her eyes and said resolutely, "… and if you have to, ensure that there is no way that the documents can be traced back to you."

~

Two nights and three days zoomed past. Time had a way of fleeting when the two were together. It would be nine weeks by the time they'd meet next. Saying goodbyes was expectedly hard.

They made love in silence. Soft caresses and tender kisses planted over each other's bodies as they combined fluidly into one another. The act itself expressing a thousand words that each wanted to say, but was unable to.

Hope juxtaposed angst as Nitya boarded the bus to Pune later that day.

LVIII

"This is an absolute disaster! We are so fucked!!" Ram bellowed as he threw the print-out that had just been handed over to him. He stood up with his fists resting on the desk. The girl from PR had not expected this outburst from her usually calm and composed Head of Marketing. "We need to have some kind of mitigation plan and response drafted before the US is up. Find out who the hell this Rhea whatever her last name is and figure out if there is any way this story can be buried. This shall spiral should others in the media latch on to this story. It will not take much for them to understand that the 'Mumbai headquartered IT hardware multi-national' is us."

"Ram, PostFacto.com is run by Saugato Sen," the girl from PR braved on. "It's the online news portal of Facts First TV Network. They launched it a couple of months back. You'd skipped the launch event, remember? If anyone, it is you who can pick up the phone and talk to Saugato."

"Going directly to him would mean acceptance of the story as fact. Any concern portrayed by me would also imply us…" Ram slipped into thought as he picked up the print-out and started reading the story again, "Think of something else." He hollered as she closed the door after her. He picked up his desk telephone and punched the keys purposefully.

"Rishi, I need you in my cabin. Pronto!"

Rishi luckily had seen the storm clouds from a distance. Seeing the PR girl with Ram had set his bells ringing. He rushed to Ram's cabin. He'd already read Rhea's article. He had not really expected this magnitude of a reaction from Ram. At least not with the very first one.

They probably have no idea that it's a series!

'More Than What Meets the Eye at DGIT' the article's headline had screamed and the sub-heading was, *'Hardware Firms Possibly Involved'*. The article went on to describe the CVC raid at the DGIT. It talked about 'sources' having confirmed that a tender was indeed in the offing for procuring a very large requirement of IT hardware. Rhea had cleverly left it to the readers' imagination to figure out whether the so-called source was indeed the whistleblower. The article raised questions regarding possible mismanagement and underhand dealings related to the tender. It mentioned in passing that certain 'high-ranking officials of a Mumbai headquartered IT hardware firm' had met the Director General a few weeks before the raid.

"Hi! You want to discuss the projections for the Montara transition right?" Rishi asked Ram feigning any knowledge or awareness.

"No. Sit down!" his demeanour contradicted the calm Ram tried to project with his tone.

"Read this."

Rishi picked up the print-out that Ram had pushed towards his end of the desk. He took his time reading it, mindful of Ram's impatient tapping of the table with his fingernails.

"Well," Ram asked expectantly.

"They cannot trace anything related to the tender back to us

Ram. I always shared the drafts of the tender specifications that I created in hard copy form. Modifications as and when were always made in parallel on their desktop computer and my notebook." Rishi said confidently. "I must mention here that I always felt that Vinod was a dodgy character," he added referring to one of the officers who had assisted in preparing the tender.

Rishi didn't think there was any reason for Ram to suspect that he had any role to play here. However, just in case Ram did want to find out whether Rishi had anything to do with Rhea's article mentioning the meeting, Rishi had slipped in Vinod's name. With that, Rishi hoped he had been successful in keeping the needle of suspicion safely pointing away from him.

At least for a while!

Rishi was not sure whether Ram even knew the extent of the mess. He knew for a fact that Ram had refused Prasanna's request for adjusting the amount required for the kickback from the marketing budgets. What he didn't know was whether Ram knew that it had been arranged for. He desperately wanted to go and tell him about the money that was supposed to be paid to the Director General and how the money did in fact come into the country. Basically, the entire story. He stopped himself from doing so. Out of sheer respect for him, Rishi wanted to believe that Ram had no part to play.

Ram broke Rishi's thoughts by dropping a bombshell.

"Prasanna is going to be in town tomorrow and the day after. He is here for the ILT meeting," he said referring to the monthly India Leadership Team meeting. It was not usual for Prasanna to attend the meeting in person. He typically would join through video conferencing.

"I am going to ask Tubby, to set up a meeting first thing in the morning," he said referring to Tabassum, the PR girl. "Prasanna should be in by nine, he's taking the first flight out from Delhi. I want to spend an hour with him, you and Tubby. Cannot let this article tarnish ICI."

Tubby walked in without bothering to knock. "Prasanna has confirmed. I connected with Rhea Bahadur. She stands by her article. Says she has verified the entry register and has proof that a team from ICI was there at the DGIT and had indeed met the Director General. I think she has access to someone inside DGIT."

Ram turned and gave Rishi an acknowledging glance.

"Also," Tubby continued, "some other news networks reached out. They are just fishing right now but…"

"Talk to the agency. Draft a release and keep it ready. We should just say that Steve was in the country and that it was a courtesy visit to a large account. One of five others that he made. Routine. Throw in some numbers, large bids that we have won and supplied to various Government undertakings. End with how we are committed to the highest levels of business ethics, etc. I want the draft on my table by close of business today."

~

Later that evening, Rishi caught an interview of Rhea on Saugato's prime time news show. The scroll on the screen read 'No Smoke Without Fire'.

Indeed!

LVIX

Prasanna was already in the office by the time Rishi reached. He was sitting in Ram's cabin. Rishi contemplated walking in and saying hello but decided against it. As Rishi settled in at his desk and powered up his notebook, he felt a tap on his shoulder.

"What? No saying hello to your ex-boss is it?"

Rishi was astonished. It was uncharacteristic of Prasanna on two counts. Not many would have seen Prasanna in a cheerful mood—he was the archetypal grumpy boss! Two, it was even rarer for him to walk up to someone and say hello—he was too smug for it.

"Ha ha! Not at all, I was just getting ready for our meeting. Wasn't aware you'd arrived."

"Good to see you, man! I was just on my way outside for a quick smoke. Care to join me?"

Rishi agreed. He did not have a choice in the matter. Prasanna would have literally dragged him, he already had Rishi firmly in his grip.

The smoking area was a small balcony with garden furniture and ashbins. It was green with high Areca Palms lining the perimeter and a water body with a cascade to one side. The Mumbai sea breeze constantly flushing out the overhang of lit tobacco. Funny as it sounded, the smoking area actually gave a feeling of freshness!

Prasanna offered Rishi a cigarette and a light. He lit his own, took a deep first drag, and said, "I hope you haven't told Ram anything about your little trip to Muzaffarnagar." The friendliness in him from just a few minutes ago dissolving in air along with smoke he blew out.

"Bear in mind what I told you about success Rishi."

Rishi did not respond. He knew better not to engage. There was a plan and it was working as of now.

"It's time guys," Ram called out.

~

As it turned out, the meeting was Ram's pretext to get Prasanna to divulge more details about the DGIT tender and the role ICI had to play. The idea was to prep the PR machinery for the next salvo. Tubby was certain that there was more coming from the PostFacto.com side.

Prasanna insisted that no further progress had been made on the Director General's ask once Ram had turned down his request for adjusting the amount from the marketing budgets. Rishi had kept his gaze fixed on Prasanna all this while. Prasanna did not blink an eyelid as he told Ram what Rishi knew to be a blatant lie. Not to say that he had expected any different!

Rishi felt as though he was stuck with a question of scruples and he didn't like the answer card that he had drawn! Now, he just had to play on!

Trust the plan!

"Did we actually plan on paying the…," Tubby hesitated as she asked perhaps weighing the word she was about to use before she actually did, "… kickback?"

Ram shrugged. It perhaps was meant to indicate his acknowledgement but not his consent.

"It is what it is," Prasanna got up. "I think we are done here," he turned to Tubby, "Just issue that release and we should be fine."

"We have things to discuss," Prasanna wrapped his knuckles on Ram's table as he made his way out.

First blood!

LX

Unplanned and more importantly unexpected! The event and the content took Rishi by surprise. It was barely five in the morning when Rishi's cell phone rang. As he picked up the phone, he noticed that he had over a dozen text messages that had arrived through the course of the night.

It was Nitya.

"He was here!" she said. Rishi could sense both the anger and frustration in her voice.

"Sunny was here last week," she exclaimed.

I knew it wasn't just the ILT meeting that got him to come to Mumbai!

"The judge had insisted on his presence for all future hearings. His lawyers have filed a grievance that the court has insisted on them filing objections to my plea for granting a divorce. They have given an application requesting the court to make an endeavour at reconciliation. Apparently some section or sub-section of the Hindu Marriage Act that makes it incumbent on the court to first attempt a reconciliation."

Rishi figured that Nitya had been up all night and the text messages waiting to be read in his inbox were the ones she would have sent through the night. He was acutely aware that comforting Nitya over a telephone line was not going to be easy.

"Calm down Nitya,"

Again, it was not going to be easy. Nitya had a head start. She had been ruminating all night!

"Next they are going to demand visitation rights," Nitya continued her outburst. Rishi's preliminary attempt at consolation obviously had failed.

"We knew about this," Rishi continued, remounting his efforts to ebb the flow from the other side. "They are going to use all the available moves to either stall or get your plea thrown out Nitya. We discussed this. In fact, you were the one who told me all this last time."

"Yeah! But why must he do this? Why can he not just leave me be?"

Rishi knew it was time to change his prescription. He realised that it is not always that a man has to play the knight in shining armour! There are times when the woman is not looking to be rescued. She does not want a solution to her problem. All that she wants, is a patient ear.

He did just that.

Ten minutes later, as they ended the call, with a much relieved and calmer Nitya, he uttered his next set of words. Just five of them, "I am here for you."

DELHI

~

Ab Door Nahin![II]

LXI

Delhi! It was home and so it always felt like one. Even when the circumstances were, let's say, challenging. Rishi took a deep breath of the evening air as he alighted the aircraft. There had been developments during the past week that had necessitated his visit. Prasanna had been the catalyst that exacerbated them.

~

"Prasanna told the ILT that he'd prefer that you were present in Delhi to 'handle' things at the DGIT," Ram gestured. What he had just delivered in the form of information, was at heart, an instruction. "Don't worry, your role here is safe. This is just until the storm blows over."

The marching orders had been with immediate effect. Rhea had fired her next salvo. The saving grace as far as Ram and ICI were concerned was that the article mentioned ICI's complete denial of any wrongdoing in the matter. A link to the press release issued by ICI had been provided.

The article, however, went deeper into the hypothesis that there were aspects of the CVC raid on the DGIT that begged question. Rhea had made good use of the conversation she'd had with Rishi to weave the possibilities around how the tender may have been rigged.

This time around the probing questions were for the internal ways of working of the Director General's Office. Sources again were quoted as saying how the point two percent 'V' signal was widely understood, accepted, and propagated by the staff. Given the rampant levels of corruption, the article opined that procurements dating back to the start of the Director General's tenure were under a cloud.

Rishi's mandate was clear. He was to engage with the officials in the DGIT, if possible, figure out the 'sources' and ideally, plug the leaks to prevent further damage to ICI's reputation.

The expectation per se made Rishi extremely happy about how highly his capability and hold over the account was being rated in the top echelons. That was the naïve Rishi inside him. The street smart and now hardened professional Rishi in him kept insisting that he was being used. He once again had managed to get embroiled in a power tussle amongst the ILT members. He was the lamb that was being used to lure the lion!

He understood that he needed to tread the road ahead with caution. Too much attention on ICI and this could end up blowing on his face entirely. Not enough and the audit guys would ensure that there were consequences of the process violations that took place. All the pieces of the plan needed to fall in place just right for the external media heat to cook Prasanna.

Now that he was in Delhi, he had a better chance of controlling the course of things.

It will work!

LXII

It was the three of them after a while. Rishi had not read anything into Abhi's "Are you sure you want to meet up at Bhattu's?" remark when he'd called to make plans. It was a Friday evening. With a cleverly engineered "I miss your cooking Amma" early dinner with his parents out of the way, Rishi was ready and looking forward to a drink with his buddies. Mr. and Mrs. Krishnamurthy were the early to bed kinds. Although they did not really like it, they throughout Rishi's engineering life had gotten used to their son disappearing shortly after his arrival.

~

Friendship is a lot like listening to your favourite song. No matter where, when, and how many times you press pause, you still can press play and continue to hum along as though you'd never paused!

Somehow, that particular night was not hitting the right notes. Friendship is also about feeling anything but awkward. There was an elephant in the room and it needed to be acknowledged. As usual, it required Abhi's bluntness.

"Tum saale kitty party wali Aunties ki tarah PC karte rahoge ya mudde pe aaoge?" he said, admonishing Bhattu and Rishi for wasting the evening with polite conversation much like ladies at a kitty party.

Rishi wondered why he hadn't taken note of Bhattu's unusual reticence. He realised that he had been too pre-occupied with telling his own story.

He got up, put his drink down, and stood with his arms open, inviting a hug. Bhattu perhaps had already sensed what Rishi was about to do. There was only a microsecond of a delay in his acceptance.

"Dude... I... it... it just happened"

"Sshh..." Rishi tightened the hug as he shushed Bhattu.

"Hey! Don't you guys dare leave me out of this," Abhi jumped in to complete the group hug.

There are times when you do not need to speak. Times when your body communicates way more than what words could have. Times when silence speaks!

"Now I know why you fuckers kept insisting that she was not right for me," Rishi said breaking away from the hug and picking his drink.

"Not I dude, it was always this guy," Bhattu countered.

"Yeah! Look how that seems to have worked out! Great! Isn't it? " Abhi jibed sarcastically, as he raised his glass.

"Through thick and thin!" they said in unison.

The night regained its spirit!

It was Bhattu's turn now as he recounted how he'd realised what he felt for Rhea was something more than concern.

"Saala! Vaise hi har jagah line lagata tha. Tere jaate hi chaloo ho

gaya." Abhi trained his guns on Bhattu as he guilt-tripped him for flirting with Rhea once Rishi had left for Mumbai.

Bhattu acknowledged that Abhi had been extremely supportive of the two getting together.

"I'm genuinely happy Bhattu! Rhea is a great girl. Maybe at some level, Abhi was right. Just that it was not she who wasn't right for me. It was me who wasn't right for her."

Bhattu mock punched Rishi. "Don't."

"Oho! Fagrette on karo!" Abhi implored Rishi to light the cigarette he'd been holding all this while. He also wanted Bhattu and Rishi to move on and stop moping.

Abhi had yet again used the nonsensical to make sense!

LXIII

"She's taking it too far Saugato!" Rishi could imagine an all worked up Ram glowering at the other end of the conference line. Tubby had set up the call. Prasanna and Rishi had dialled-in from Delhi, Ram and Tubby had connected from Mumbai whilst Saugato who was travelling had joined the call from a business lounge at some airport. Ram had used all his clout to ensure Saugato was on that call.

~

The third in the investigative series had been published online the previous evening. Rhea's article this time had moved beyond corruption into the realm of crime!

Rhea had interviewed the chief investigating officer of the Anees Chaudhry murder case. The officer confirmed that the trail had gone cold and though the case was still open, the police were leaning towards attributing the crime to an inter-gang rivalry. The artist sketches of the alleged shooters matched those of known contract killers Ravi and Munna who were in hiding ever since.

That was the part that was already in the public domain. It was the part regarding the investigation of the economic offence that was being reported for the first time. Now with the enactment of the FEMA – a law that had sharper teeth, all *hawala* cases were being investigated with renewed fervour.

The diary that had been confiscated at Anees Chaudhry's had entries regarding a *hawala* for a payment from the United States. The delivery of *bees*[45] *peti*[46] to a person based in Delhi whose name had not been divulged was the last entry in the diary and dated the day of the murder! Furthermore, it was suspected that the transaction could have been carried out for some kind of corporate entity. This inference had been drawn on the basis of the statement by the teenager who had been picked up for questioning. The boy, in his statement, had mentioned that the young men who had come to collect the money were speaking with each other in English.

Rhea's article once again raised questions regarding the timing of the raid, the DGIT tender, and the alleged *hawala* tracing back to the US. Circumstantial evidence that pieced together hitherto unrelated events. Taking it too far according to Ram.

Saugato was a tough nut. He did not crack. He had been very no-nonsense. He said his team had already published ICI's statement and there was nothing further they could do. From a journalistic perspective, he said that there was no questioning the veracity of the articles that had already been published. He spoke of the high standards of ethics his organisation maintained and even slipped in a marketing line, "We place Facts First," as he had diplomatically closed the call.

Prasanna was on tenterhooks all through it and was not to be seen post the conference call.

~

Rishi too was finding walking this tightrope tough. Every waking moment, he could not help but think that though he

---

[45] The number twenty in Hindi.
[46] A colloquial reference to One Lakh Rupees, typically used by the underworld.

was a part of the plan, he still risked becoming a part of it – as a consequence!

As the series had unfolded, the gravitas had increased. The depth and detail that Rhea was bringing to her pieces were fetching her wide acclaim. She had researched her angles really well. Something that made Rishi realise the reason Rhea had been confident about the plan from day one.

~

"Well done! Must admit that you have even me running scared now," Rishi said as he sipped his coffee.

"Saugato told me about the call," Rhea replied as she put the cell phone down. She had just finished sending a text message. "So? What are we supposed to be talking about?"

"Well… Ram gave me a call after the conference call with Saugato had ended. He said that Saugato had suggested, and he had readily agreed, that someone from ICI should be speaking with you. That way ICI could be working 'with' you to give the ICI perspective."

"Yeah, same! A warning though, Saugato told me that I shall continue to have control. I am to hear you out and that is all," Rhea said categorically.

"No arguments there. I'm with you on that one. I'll toe the line. Just keep feeding the same to Tubby just so Ram doesn't get suspicious. As far as I am concerned, it gives me a reason to be talking to you. Just imagine, if they were to find out that we are acquainted and that you are dating my best friend."

"Or…"

Rishi knew what was coming! He cursed himself.

"… worse… they find out that we used to date each other. No wait were engaged!" she stubbed out the cigarette she was smoking into the ashtray and reached to light one more. He really had her agitated.

"I… I'm sorry Rhea," Rishi said choosing his words carefully, "I did not mean to distance myself from our past. It was beautiful. I ruined it. It genuinely makes me happy to see you with Bhattu. All that I wanted to do, was to respect your present."

"I am sorry too. I overreacted," Rhea took a deep drag and passed the cigarette to Rishi. She had flicked away the momentary spurt of anger that she would've felt along with the ash.

Phew!

Rhea indicated that she had two more articles lined up for the series. She shared what Rishi had suspected all this while. The Director General and his officers had struck similar deals with other key manufacturers. They had ensured that the very design of the tender that was to be floated and its technical requirements were such that multiple vendors could qualify. Global IT hardware major PBM and the home-grown manufacturer of computers Swadeshi Computers also had the DG on the take. None could have known that aspect better than Rishi!

Rhea also confirmed what Rishi had long believed to be just an urban legend amongst the IT hardware sales guys. Swadeshi Computers, during its initial days of operation, had apparently paid its way to receive an order from one of the Ministries. It was the end of the Financial Year and Swadeshi Computers needed to ensure delivery of a thousand or so computers to the Ministry. However, they were yet to ramp up their assembly capabilities for the Central Processing Unit (CPU) to match the tight timelines associated with the delivery. To ensure that the order was retained with them, Swadeshi Computers went ahead and shipped a consignment with the keyboard, the monitors, some boxes containing the processing units they were able to produce and to make up for the shortfall, they shipped the cartons with bricks inside! The DGIT in cohorts with complying ministry officials then helped get the consignment rejected on technical grounds. The entire lot was then taken back by Swadeshi Computers. The actual supply of the CPU's as per 'requisite specifications' happened six weeks later!

"The take is point two percent, but the rot is one hundred percent!"

Rishi oddly felt safe in knowing it wasn't just his neck of the woods that was on fire. It was the entire fucking forest!

LXIV

"I am coming to Delhi tomorrow. Ibbani is also coming with me. We'll be staying at the Park Royal. Don't ask me why. I shall do the explaining once I am there. Can you squeeze in lunch with us tomorrow?"

"Of course! I'll be there at the airport to pick you up. That way we get more time together."

"Don't bother. It's been arranged for. More later. See you at two!"

It was past midnight, but there was no way Rishi could have put it down as a distress call. If anything, it was very to the point, reminiscent of the Nitya of engineering days. However, that feeling did not prevent Rishi from wondering about the development. Questions kept bubbling up in his mind all through the night. Why the sudden decision to come to Delhi? Why come with Ibbani? Was it something related to work or with the divorce proceedings? How long was she going to be in the city? Would she be meeting Prasanna? The mishmash of thoughts added further chaos to thoughts regarding the DGIT affair pre-occupying him.

Rishi knew that there was little else that he could do. Except for waiting!

~

He did not have any further meetings lined up. Rishi had just spent the morning typing out a long e-mail to Ram and Tubby. That had promptly led to a quick phone call that outlined the next steps on managing the agenda with PostFacto.com and DGIT. The 'containment strategy' as Tubby kept referring to it as.

Prasanna had called in sick and hadn't come to the office. It was nearing two. Rishi told the office accountant that he was done for the day and left.

The hotel Nitya had picked was a stone's throw away from Rishi's office. He decided to walk down. As he walked, the thought that crossed his mind was that the hotel was a bit too close to the office. At least for his comfort.

Or maybe, comfort was the intent!

~

Nitya along with Ibbani was already in the restaurant waiting for Rishi to arrive.

"Sorry, I ordered. Ibby gets feisty when she's hungry!"

"Ello!" she said, with all the excitement and enthusiasm of a two-year-old.

Rishi took his seat across the table, his gaze fixed on the little angel. He had seen pictures before but this was the first time he was meeting her.

She was sitting on a baby chair, yoghurt smeared all over her; extending from her mouth all the way up to her chubby cheeks. She was wearing a bright yellow frock with big white polka dots. The little bib that Nitya would have tied around her neck had not prevented food from reaching the frock. Rishi was overwhelmed.

"I had imagined my first meeting with Ibby differently…"

"Should have done it long ago. I am sorry I delayed it," Nitya cut in. "I thought long and hard about our conversation the other day. In fact, about how little you had to say in that conversation and how much that little meant for me. The impact it had on me!"

Lunch arrived.

"I decided I had waited long enough and the world needed to know what I felt. I had denied myself that right once already. I wanted to be able to live free."

Rishi helped himself to a serving.

Nitya attended to Ibby, who by now, had finished both eating and playing with her food. By the time she had finished her lunch and had Ibby cleaned up, Rishi too was done eating.

"Let's go upstairs," Nitya said as she signed for the lunch.

"May I?" Rishi volunteered to carry Ibby.

"She already has a mind of her own. If the past thirty minutes are an indicator. I think Ibby views you as a friend. She usually is not so forthcoming with her 'Ello'," Nitya stepped aside.

~

Ibby had readily allowed Rishi to carry her. They were in the room. Nitya had tucked in Ibby. It was time for her afternoon nap.

Nitya had been itching to continue the conversation. "So…" she began, taking her seat opposite Rishi on the couch that was lining the large window with the vista of the Baha'i temple.

"… I decided to tell all concerned that I was in love! I started with Appa and Amma and told them just that. They wanted to know who it was and I told them that as well," Nitya paused, waiting for a reaction from Rishi.

"And?" was all Rishi could manage to say. This day was turning out to be overwhelming in different ways!

The monosyllabic response from Rishi was sufficient for Nitya to continue.

"Then I pondered on whether to and if I do go ahead, how much to tell Sunny."

But, why now? Why risk the divorce proceedings?

Rishi knew the answer was coming up, he just wasn't sure it would be the right one!

"Sunny had communicated through his lawyer to check if we would consider a request to delay the next hearing by a few weeks. Ostensibly commitments related to work."

Ibbani stirred in her sleep interrupting Nitya's flow. She went and sat next to her on the bed. She gently stroked her back to sleep.

"My lawyer suggested it would be a good thing if I were to pay a visit along with Ibby. You know… check things out myself. Also, to see if spending some time with Ibby would make Sunny change his mind with regard to the plea that is pending," she said, as she walked back and sat next to him on the couch.

So did you?

"He was supposed to meet us at the airport and we were to have breakfast together. However, by the time we touched down he'd sent a text inviting us over. Said he wasn't feeling well. His driver was waiting at the airport with a placard."

"Yes, I heard. He'd called in sick at work too," Rishi said in a very matter-of-fact manner, not wanting to let his response betray his actual thoughts and anxiousness to know what had transpired.

"He has been to Pune a few times since Ibby was born. Sunny is a different person when she's around. Extremely calm and loving. Makes you wonder how the same person is capable of being so aggressive and hurtful…" she trailed off. Rishi placed his hand on her thigh reassuringly.

"When we met this morning, I told him what I have been telling him all this while. That there was no possibility of a reconciliation. I told him that all this time apart had made me realise one thing for sure. What I'd felt for him wasn't really love. It was perhaps just a weird alignment of ambitions that I mistook for love…" she paused.

Nitya gazed out of the window thinking.

"I also told him that I have only ever fallen in love once, and that was while I was doing my engineering," she said.

She took Rishi's hand, held it between her palms, and planted a kiss.

"Life has given me a second chance, I am not going to let it pass me by."

LXV

To say that the ten days that Nitya spent in Delhi were eventful would be putting it mildly. Things got an unexpected fillip as far as Nitya and Rishi were concerned. Nevertheless, it wasn't all easy going. At least, not the way things started.

Prasanna had not sought the details of who it was that Nitya wanted a future with. He however did share with Nitya that he'd just gone along with his lawyers when they told him about the plea they were filing on his behalf. He admitted to her that he hadn't considered reconciliation as a possibility. That said, he certainly wanted a chance. What he also told her, was that he wanted a fair shot at being a father to Ibbani. Something, that he felt Nitya had denied him thus far.

Prasanna was going to fight every bit of the way to assert his rights as a father. It was a game that Nitya had started but he was willing to play it and win in his words, "At any cost."

Rishi understood that part very well.

~

"Ennamopa! On ishtam," said Mrs. Krishnamurthy in her exasperation. Her sad and defeated tone implying there was not much that she could do. After all, as she had put it, it was his life and his decision to make.

He had to tell them. There wasn't ever going to be a right time for telling them. Of course, the fact that Nitya was in town with Ibbani did have a role to play. However, those were not the circumstances that had led to the discussion.

Regardless of how deep your friendship runs, friends have a knack for springing the most unwelcome surprises on you. It was actually a phone call. No! Make that two phone calls. One from Bhattu's parents and the other from the Bahadurs that started it all. Both had called to invite Mr. and Mrs. Krishnamurthy to bless the children. Bhattu and Rhea were getting engaged!

Rishi couldn't possibly have taken his parents through the why and what of his break-up with Rhea. Explaining how Bhattu and Rhea ended up together would have been a whole new nightmare!

As far as Rishi was concerned, the Krishnamurthys as his parents had the appetite for just one calamity. He unleashed the one with the most far-reaching impact!

"I realised that I was in love with someone else Amma."

He started at the very beginning. The first time that he saw her. He talked about participating in all the festivals and how his fondness for Nitya had grown. How torn he'd felt when it all ended prematurely. About how he ran into her at a conference in Mumbai. Her failed marriage, Ibbani, everything!

He had not expected them to accept everything right away. Yes, he hoped that they'd understand or at least try to. Rishi always had believed that of the two, his mother was more broad-minded. However, his hopes took a beating when Mrs. Krishnamurthy focussed on Nitya's marital status and Ibbani.

"Athai vidu Vaidehi! Thala ezhuthu ennavo, athu dhaan nadakkum," the pragmatic scientist once again came to Rishi's rescue with his timely use of profound philosophy in Tamil. He asked his wife to accept things the way they were. Reminding her of the adage, 'That which is fated, shall indeed happen!'

In that moment Rishi realised one thing. In his life, help somehow had always arrived from unexpected quarters. He had never really acknowledged or understood who his guardian angels were. All his life he'd heard his father say that he was destined for bigger things. Rishi was almost twenty-eight now! Yet, he was pleasantly surprised by his father's support in the matter. In fact, encouraged by his father's unfailing belief in what fate had in store for him.

"When are we meeting the love of your life then?" Mr. Krishnamurthy turned around and asked Rishi. He was too filled with emotion for any words to have come out. He went ahead and gave his father a hug. Something he couldn't remember having ever done. Something he should have done long before!

Mrs. Krishnamurthy too, even if somewhat grudgingly, nodded her head. Amma had an 'I'm interested' look on her face now. It had been piqued by the next level that had been reached in an otherwise plateauing father-son relationship!

The decision had now been conclusively made!

~

Nitya was charm personified that day. She had the Krishnamurthys floored within minutes! Rishi liked this feeling. For the first time in many, many years, he mumbled a quiet prayer as he passed by the *puja*[47] area in the kitchen.

Amma had not spared any effort in laying out an elaborate South Indian spread. It even included a non-spicy fare for the little visitor!

By evening Nitya had regaled Mr. and Mrs. Krishnamurthy with anecdotes from engineering. Ibby had taken a liking to Rishi's father and kept him company with her antics while Nitya and Mrs. Krishnamurthy got acquainted.

"I have tidied the guest room. Why don't you and Ibby stay the night?"

That invitation from Mrs. Krishnamurthy to Nitya bore testament to the amount of progress relationships could make in a single day. How personalities could surmount perceptions and pre-conceived notions.

If only people just heard each other out!

---

[47] Prayer

LXVI

He never would have imagined himself doing it. Yet there he was in the middle of the night signing documents as a part of the admission formalities. Rishi paused to think about what should be filled under the 'relationship with the patient' column.

Rishi had last spoken with Prasanna that evening. It had been the usual Prasanna checking with him about the developments on the DGIT front. The heat was getting to him. He was getting roasted not only on account of the unwanted media attention that ICI was drawing but also, by the progress made by the GIA team in terms of the audit. The India Leadership Team had dipped in its credibility rating and Prasanna, it could be said, was to blame. The global leadership was now looking for fall guys. The troika that had met the Director General along with Rishi was in the line of fire. Prasanna's need to vent it out possibly explained the call he had placed to Rishi.

He had not been coming to the office the past week. Nitya had visited him a couple of times to drop Ibby off. She too had mentioned that he'd looked a bit pale.

~

It was Sethu, Prasanna's man Friday who had requested the hospital authorities to call Rishi. He had the presence of mind to drive Prasanna to a hospital as soon as he'd complained of acute pain in his abdomen. Prasanna had been taken to the emergency ward. Sethu however, had been unable to go through the admission process on his own. He was Prasanna's driver, cook, household help all rolled into one. He had met Rishi more than a few times. He was aware that he stayed close by.

"Attendant of Prasanna Seshadri!" one of the nurses from the emergency ward called out.

Sethu nodded a request for Rishi to go, "*Bhaiyya aapko samajh aayega,*" he said indicating that Rishi would understand what the nurse had to say better. He stepped back allowing Rishi to proceed towards the ward.

Prasanna was on one of the beds in the far corner of the ward. As Rishi walked in with the nurse, the attending doctor walked across.

"You are?"

"Rishi, I am a colleague. Prasanna doesn't have any relatives in Delhi."

"Okay. Based on all the indications we are suspecting pancreatitis. We have taken samples for running some tests. I hope you have completed the admission process."

Rishi nodded a yes.

"We'll be putting him on intravenous fluids and might be keeping him here for a few days. Your colleague seems to have ignored the early symptoms."

He explained the situation as he had understood it to Sethu. Rishi immediately called Amma, told her about the developments, and requested her to pack a bag for him with a few essentials, a change of clothes, and keep it ready for Sethu to pick it up. Since this was going to be a long haul he needed to access Prasanna's insurance details. Sethu, fortunately, had the card with him, Prasanna had asked him to keep it.

~

Prasanna was now in the hospital room. The IV fluid drip had been set up next to him and his vitals were being monitored. Sethu had left. Rishi was alone in the room with Prasanna.

He looked at him as he settled himself on the attendant's couch. Rishi could tell that Prasanna was still in substantial pain. Prasanna looked at Rishi and signalled for him to come closer.

Perhaps there was something he wanted to say. Whatever it was, Prasanna could not get himself to say it. He started drifting away. Nonetheless, Rishi sensed it.

"Don't you worry, we'll get you out of this," Rishi said as he held Prasanna's hand in his.

LXVII

"*Chutiya ho gaya hai tu!*" Abhi was furious. He believed that Rishi had lost his mind. They were all sitting in the hospital canteen. Rishi had called and informed Abhi. Bhattu and Rhea had come too. Bhattu had got dinner packed at home for Rishi since he was staying the night at the hospital.

"That man is solely responsible for all the strife you have in your life currently," Abhi growled trying to communicate his frustration while keeping his voice down.

"He does not have anyone he can call family guys! He's all alone!" Rishi muttered.

"Abhi does have a point," Bhattu concurred. "That driver cum cook of his… he can stay. Why do you need to? It is one thing to check in on him but staying here as his attendant! Sorry, I don't understand it either."

"You are doing the right thing Rishi, don't you worry about getting validation from these two." Rhea became the lone voice of reassurance.

"Have you spoken with Nitya yet?"

Nitya had just left a day earlier. Rishi had contemplated telling her but had held back informing her till the course of treatment had been decided by the doctors attending Prasanna. Also, she had left Delhi in high spirits. Perhaps, after a very long time!

He did not want to spoil it for her. He also knew that he could not hold off informing her for very long either.

The five of them had spent a couple of evenings together. Abhi, Bhattu, and now Rhea were a part of the extended family. After all, friends are the family you can choose!

The three of them kept him company at the hospital. While Bhattu and Rhea left once the visiting hours had closed, Abhi had lingered on till late.

Despite their obvious reservations regarding Rishi's decision to attend to Prasanna; Rishi was glad that he had their complete and unquestioned support.

He was going to need it!

LXVIII

"Trust me! You are better off there in Pune. It will be too much of a burden for you to manage things here with Ibby around." Rishi had been speaking with Nitya every night and giving her updates about Prasanna's condition.

~

It had been a roller coaster ride up until now and there seemed to be no end in sight. Prasanna's condition had worsened by the second day and he had to be taken in for surgery. His gall bladder had developed an infection due to the formation of gallstones and had to be removed. Prasanna's condition had improved after the surgery and he had been stable for almost three days thereafter.

In between the running around for the surgery, the frequent tests, collecting the test reports, and then consulting specialist doctors, Rishi and Prasanna in his quasi-conscious state had conversations as well. Not very long ones but. Prasanna simply did not have the energy for them. In some measure, even though minuscule, they'd made an attempt to get to know each other as people.

The topics of discussion would be random.

On one of the better days; days where he would remain conscious for more than a few minutes and not writhe in constant pain; Rishi found Prasanna with tears rolling down his cheeks. His bed had been propped up by one of the nurses to allow him a seated position.

"I have never discussed this with anyone."

Rishi looked at Prasanna inquisitively.

"I have a daughter. She'll be turning three soon. I got to spend some time with her before this happened," he started slipping into a reverie, maybe it was the sedatives kicking in. He fought it.

"Best days in a long while man." He seemed to be reminiscing. "In a very long while!" He stretched the word to make his point.

"I am aware," Rishi said. He was contemplative.

"I have been keeping Nitya updated," Rishi told Prasanna after giving what he was about to say, some thought.

"She was a senior at college. We both are from H.I.T, Mandya. It was much later that I found out that the two of you used to be married."

"Still are..." Prasanna interjected. "Still are," he mumbled again. "Still are," and again.

Rishi was not too sure whether Prasanna was talking to himself or he had meant for Rishi to hear it.

~

They never went back to that conversation. They also did not get much time to get back to it. Prasanna developed post-surgical complications. His ultrasound had indicated an infection. Less than a week after he'd been operated upon, Prasanna was wheeled into the operation theatre for the second time.

It was going to be a time taking procedure. Apparently an extremely delicate procedure that involved scraping off the bits of infected tissue from the surface of the pancreas and if need be, the liver.

LXIX

Meanwhile, outside the hospital, the media storm had now gained in intensity. There were a dozen newspapers, media houses, and PIL[48] filing lawyers baying for blood. Rhea's final piece had now been published online. It was the last nail in the coffin as far as the Director General was concerned. His resignation while still under suspension made the headlines the day after PostFacto.com had published Rhea's article. His was the first of many resignations that followed. The exits were not limited to the DGIT alone, a few officers in a particular ministry of the government too followed suit.

~

There had been some developments in the ICI world as well.

"Your work in Delhi is pretty much done Rishi. You can come back to Mumbai now," Ram told him over the telephone. "The focus of the stories, for now, has shifted on to accountability of those holding top government offices. Thanks to you, Tubby has developed a reasonably good working relationship with Rhea and she can take it forward from here."

"I'll need some time Ram. A week or two more at least. I can use my leave if need be. Prasanna needs me here."

That there was no love lost between Ram and Prasanna was well known. Ram, however, could not fault Rishi. He had just

---

[48] Public Interest Litigation

given a display of courage and character. A trait that was rare, almost bordering extinction in the professional context.

"That'll not be necessary. We can spare you for two weeks. See you on the monthly projections call."

The ongoing audit investigations had led to significant changes in some of the processes being followed at ICI. The Product Management teams of each of the countries needed to submit their projections to the Global Supply Chain team on the third Friday of each calendar month. The GSC would then do their material resource planning and revert with the supply volumes and timelines for the country teams to comment upon.

The projections call was essentially a mechanism to make the forecasting process transparent to all the ICI teams across the world and to balance the demand-supply. It was also a rap on the knuckles for the ICI India team!

Gone were the days when India could spring surprises in their projections. The component inventory pile up on account of DGIT had made a significant dent in operating margins. It had set a vicious cycle in motion. ICI eventually ended up delaying its new product launches till the excess inventories had been consumed. Consequently, the revenues and market share had to take a beating, which in turn, ended up eroding a significant amount of market capital on the exchanges.

If company grapevine was to be believed the axe had indeed fallen and heads had begun to roll! The word was, that Stephen Smith had been asked to leave by the ICI board.

Rishi had long known that it was Steve who had arranged for the money to be sent from the US to India using the *hawala* route. The end seemed anear!

What remained to be seen, was who else the axe would take in its swoop as it fell!

LXX

The operation had gone well. Prasanna was shifted into the ICU for observation. His condition was now stable albeit critical. The two surgeries had taken a toll on him. According to the doctors, age was on his side as far as his convalescence was concerned, not his history!

It was the first time in two weeks that Rishi was not spending the night at the hospital. He did get a few hours every couple of days when he'd head home to freshen up, catch up on work, and sleep but, they were far from adequate. With Prasanna in the ICU the hospital staff themselves had recommended that Rishi take a break. Sethu had readily agreed to take on the role of the attendant for the night.

~

Rishi was at home speaking to Nitya. Fate had taken a few unexpected turns over the past few months. Thankfully for the two of them, they did not have to follow through on their pledge of not maintaining contact with each other while the divorce proceedings were on.

"I feel guilty putting you through all this."

"I would have done what I am doing regardless Nitya. None of this is your fault."

"I so wish I was with you right now," Nitya said ruefully. "Happy Birthday Rishi! I love you! I am never going to let you go. You know what…" she paused, "It is customary for the one celebrating their birthday to get to make a wish and receive gifts. Here I am, instead, wishing for us to be together. Silly me!" she chuckled.

"I can't wait!"

"Good thing you don't have to spend the night at the hospital. Make sure you spend your birthday with the gang. The shots are on me!"

"You bet! We're meeting for drinks later in the evening. But first, I need to get through the *aarti*[49] Amma has arranged for me. I am having an early dinner with them."

~

He had turned twenty-eight. It had taken a decade for love to have finally found him! Ten years of loving, letting go, living without, and pining for. He hadn't actually thought of it as a possibility. He'd almost resigned to the eventuality that his would be a love that was unrequited.

Not today though. Rishi's birthday had started off on a different note. A positive one. Life, in general, seemed to be headed in the direction he would have wanted it to.

It was a beautiful day Rishi had thought as he stepped out of the hospital. The hot summer air had given way to a pleasant breeze. The leaves on the trees had turned yellowish-brown, ready to fall, signalling autumn was round the corner.

He was thankful that he wasn't ending up alone and desperate on his special day. He had the blessings of his parents, eternal

---

[49] A Hindu ritual where light is offered. Typically to deities and on occasion to people to ward off evil.

love pledged to him, and the promise of an evening with friends.

Rishi couldn't have asked for anything else that would have made the day more memorable!

LXXI

Be careful what you wish for, they say. It just might come true! Perhaps Rishi too shouldn't have wondered what could have made his twenty-eighth birthday more memorable. While the pieces of Rishi's world all seemed to be coming together, the world outside was falling apart! It was a day that the world changed. Unfortunately, not for the better!

~

It was nearing seven as he entered the pub. Rishi was pretty sure Abhi, Bhattu, and Rhea had a surprise planned for him. The reason he'd been asked to reach on his own. He did get surprised. Not because friends were waiting for him to walk in through the door for them to yell "Happy Birthday!" It was in fact, the very opposite.

Rishi entered an eerily silent and seemingly empty pub! There were people, but every single one of them was gathered at the far end near the bar counter, with their eyes glued to the lone television set in the pub.

As Rishi expectantly moved towards the group, he caught a glimpse of the visuals that were playing on the screen. He could see live pictures of two towers with smoke billowing out of them. The ticker at the bottom of the screen said '*Breaking News—Second Plane Crashes into World Trade Center*'. As he walked closer, one of the towers collapsed blowing a large cloud of concrete into its surroundings! The dumbfounded crowd took a collective gasp.

Bhattu was the first to notice Rishi. He put his hand up and waved, asking him to come over to the side they were. "Unbelievable man!"

Minutes later the second tower had collapsed. The party had ended before it had begun!

LXXII

It took two weeks for Prasanna to recuperate. Rishi had been by his side all through. The doctors at the hospital had finally signed his discharge. It came attached with riders. Prasanna had been advised rest for another two weeks before he could resume office.

Rishi had wheeled him up to his car. It was with some effort that Prasanna got up from the wheelchair. Sethu offered a hand but Prasanna had shirked him away. Once on his feet he gave Rishi a tight hug and held his embrace for a while. No words were spoken.

Rishi flew back to Mumbai a couple of days later.

~

The global IT hardware industry had been massively jolted by the incidents of September Eleventh. The World Trade Centre buildings had housed the offices of PBM and Chiptel. Both organisations had lost several of their leaders to the attack.

As far as ICI was concerned, matters were still unsettled. The audit investigation had concluded. Work and life had slowly settled into the cadence of the past. While Steve had resigned as was widely being expected, there had been no word on any action taken against either Prasanna or Ram. The global teams, however, were maintaining a hawk-eye on the India operations. The India Leadership Team was still intact but they seemed to be operating with diminished authority.

Tubby had become good friends with Rishi over the duration of the DGIT fiasco. According to her, people in the global PR team had been talking about the possibility of a merger. The initial response briefing for teams across the globe had already been done. It was "No Comment". A response that said nothing while saying a lot!

The coming together of PBM and ICI would create the largest IT hardware entity globally. The merged corporation was expected to have tremendous synergies in terms of supply chains, client list, and product portfolios. It was being touted as the merger of the century by many. A large consulting house had been appointed to manage the merger and ensure due diligence.

It was Tubby's considered opinion that Ram and Prasanna had been spared the axe on this account. With Steve's resignation, the matter according to her had been effectively settled. Anything less would have prevented the germination of the merger idea and anything more would hamper further progress. Just enough had been done to tick the boxes of ethics and integrity.

~

Oddly enough, the prolonged hug from Prasanna had not changed much in terms of the relationship Rishi and he shared. Neither had Prasanna shown any further acknowledgement of gratitude nor had Rishi called him to check on how he was doing.

In honest terms, Rishi was okay with the absence of communication. Any cordiality between the two would have been hugely awkward. A strong, perhaps the only reason for Rishi being able to manage Prasanna in the hospital, had been the latter's pain killer induced delirium!

LXXIII

The last time he had met them was at an airport. He was one amongst the crowd. There had been no introductions. There had been no reason for them! Well, maybe in hindsight there was one, but it wasn't exigent, at least not the way things used to be six years ago.

Major General (Retd.) K.S. Ramanna, was every bit the high-ranking army officer that his title suggested. A highly decorated one at that. He had fought in two wars and led critical anti-insurgent operations during his career. He had been awarded the Param Vishisht Seva Medal, the Kirti Chakra, and the Vir Chakra.

He had a towering personality in the literal as well as the metaphorical sense. He stood over six feet tall and was dressed impeccably, cravat, and all. His retirement had not taken a patch away from his fitness. He had a deep baritone voice and he had as many tales as any army man could tell. And boy! Could he tell them well?

Mrs. Ramanna one could tell had mastered the art of playing the hostess. She was extremely quick on wit and quite the entertainer herself. In her own words, she had years of experience being "The COW" which was a light-hearted acronym for 'The Commanding Officers Wife'. One glance and you could tell that she was the genetic source of Nitya's good looks. She was a Kodava by descent. Rumour had it that this warrior community traced its origins back to soldiers in Alexander the Great's army. "So you see, it's not the General but my side of the pool that contributes the Greek looks," she had quipped.

Rishi did not feel the need to be made comfortable, nor was there any effort from the other end. The warmth and love of the home were such that he was comfortable from get-go! The Ramannas retirement home was an interesting mix of traditions. The house was literally sprinkled with art and handicrafts picked up all over the country. The choice of furniture was very reminiscent of the residue of Victorian culture that remains in the armed forces, especially, the army. The walls were reserved for photographs. While the sit out and the living room had photographs of Ramannas, the army family, starting with the small corridor that led to them, the inner rooms were more intimate. Happy pictures of the couple with the girls, photographs of them growing up! Ibbani's pictures were on the mantelpiece that lined the corridor.

~

He was spending the weekend in Pune. He had reached around noon. From the moment that he had arrived, either of Nitya's parents or little Ibby had kept him company.

The guest room had been kept ready for Rishi. He had been welcomed into their home.

"The new 'me' decided that it was time!" Nitya said as she walked in to tell him that the General was waiting for him at the bar. She closed the door behind her, however not fully. "Need just a little space, not secrecy," she winked as she did. They hugged and kissed. It felt lighter!

Later that evening, after they were a few drinks down and the ladies were not around, Major General Ramanna finally turned Dad! He told Rishi how happy he was that Nitya had put her failed relationship behind her. He admitted that he had his apprehensions when Nitya had told them about her growing proximity and desire to build her future with Rishi.

"A man who can so selflessly and sensitively take care of my daughter's troubled past," he'd said as he had raised his glass, "Truly, is the man Nitya deserves! Thank you, son!"

Nitya's father had said something that convinced Rishi that he had not just been welcomed into the Ramanna home, he had been welcomed into their family!

LXXIV

"That's it! It's done! I am free! Oh! I wish you were here with me right now. I desperately need a hug!" Nitya could barely suppress her excitement. It was a day before her birthday, they would have been together had it not been for the hearing. It was an important one and it did turn out to be so!

~

"He never gave me an inkling! This… this change of heart…" Nitya struggled to find the words.

They were back in the familiar confines of the hotel room. It was going to be the last time that Nitya and Rishi would be there.

"Prasanna's lawyers withdrew all the objections and pleas that they had filed. He has decided not to contest the divorce. The lawyers made the submission to the judge. They are not seeking custody either. All they requested is visitation rights. A weekend every month till she's five, or an accumulated equivalent with my explicit consent. We agreed!" She kissed Rishi.

"The decree should be available sometime next week."

He had planned it regardless, now of course they had good reason.

"What we had surely felt for each other and had held back till then was cemented on your birthday in a hotel room in Bangalore. I've never felt the same with anyone ever since, or ever!" Rishi said as he picked up the bottle of champagne from the bucket and popped it open.

He poured out two glasses and offered one to Nitya.

"Will you, Nitya Ramanna, be mine to love and to hold, till death do us part?"

"Till death do us part," she said as they clinked their glasses.

~

Their lovemaking was as sweet and effervescent as the bottle of sparkling wine they ended up polishing.

"I must caution you though," she said whimsically as she played the thought in her mind before she actually spoke the words. Nitya was lying on her side with her head resting on her palm.

"Our birthdays have had a peculiar connection with disasters. Are you sure you want to invite one upon yourself?"

"I'd choose disaster every day if it meant being with you! That would make you my damsel in distress."

"Ah… and you the knight in shining armour."

"OK, I guess we are done here with our share of cheesy teenager lines," Rishi said pulling Nitya closer.

"You started it, mister! With your champagne and your 'Till death do us part' proposal."

They laughed long and hard. It was different from all the previous occasions. There was no longer any fear of impending separation.

Time was finally a friend!

~

That weekend Rishi received an e-mail. It was from Prasanna. The subject line read 'Thank you and goodbye!' Rishi presumed it was an official e-mail and Prasanna had finally decided to move on. Once he had read a few lines, he asked Nitya to come and sit beside him.

He read out the content of the e-mail to her.

"Dear Rishi,

I have tried very hard to be able to pick up a phone and talk to you. Every time I did, I recognised that the knowledge of your presence, even if it were on the other end of a telephone line, will weigh me down. That is how indebted I feel.

Life had been spiralling downward for me. The lone silver lining in my life, appeared a few months back when I spent time with Ibbani. The more time that I spent with her, the more determined I was to fight tooth and nail for her.

Looking back, I now realise, that it is this desire of mine, the urge to capture and possess every bit of happiness and every success forever, that has been the bane of my life.

I thought about our conversations while I was in the hospital. For a large part of those conversations I was in a semi-conscious state. However, they made way to my subconscious and continued to play on my mind. They led me to my next realisation. It was you and not DJ! You are the one Nitya has always been in love with. Needless to say, I now know why!

My final realisation; you are a better man than I. Always have been.

I am not going to belittle what you have done for me by expressing my gratitude in words. Instead, I have done the one thing I could have. Ibbani and Nitya need you and your love. Moreover, your kind of love.

I shall not come in the way of things any longer.

Wish the three of you abundant happiness. Goodbye!

Prasanna

PS: There is an opportunity in the United States that I have decided to pursue. You shall be hearing more about it soon."

Rishi folded down the screen of the laptop and looked at Nitya.

"Thank you! You are the reason all this came together," she said.

"Hey!" he said as he hugged her, "We agreed we were done with the cheesy lines."

"Whatever!" she said as she blew the wisp of hair that had drifted on to her forehead.

LXXV

The wedding was an extremely cosy affair. It was family and close friends. The pomp, much to Mrs. Krishnamurthy's chagrin, had been left for the reception. The Rammanas and Mr. Krishnamurthy had gone along with Nitya and Rishi's desire for a modest wedding.

The guest list had all the usual suspects. Rhea and Bhattu came in along with Abhi. Jaya and Satya had driven down from Mumbai. While Oggy and Nutty, who were both now settled in Bangalore, had flown in together. The Ramanna family was represented by Nitya's sister and brother-in-law in addition to Ibbani and her parents.

The venue for the ceremony was the Ramanna residence in Pune. A beautiful *shamiana*[50] with a combination of white, red, and bright yellow curtains had been erected in the front lawn. It was a beautiful morning in April. The trees that surrounded the lawns were laden with flowers announcing it was springtime. The gentle breeze serving to spread their fragrance.

The one concession that had been made for Mrs. Krishnamurthy was that the wedding rituals were according to *Iyengar*[51] traditions.

---

[50] Indian ceremonial tent or awning commonly used for outdoor parties, typically weddings.
[51] An ethnoreligious group of Tamil speaking Hindu Brahmins belonging to the Vaishnava sect.

Rishi had gone with a white *kurta*[52] worn over the traditional *veshti*[53] while Nitya looked resplendent in her bright yellow silk saree with a deep red border. She was bedecked with jewellery and had the traditional floral hairdo.

The morning was packed with various rituals and much to everyone's relief some interesting games too.

Mangalyam tantunanena mama jeevana hetuna

Kanthe badhnami subhage twam jeeva sarada satam

"This auspicious thread I tie around your neck for my own well-being. O beautiful one! May you go on and live to be a hundred!" The sentiment of the mantra echoed in Rishi's mind.

The chant rented the air as Rishi tied the *mangal sutra*[54] around Nitya's neck.

---

[52] Traditional Indian upper wear akin to a shirt, usually with length ending just above the knees.
[53] Traditional Indian lower wear also known as Dhoti - A single length of white cloth wrapped around the waist.
[54] Auspicious thread tied around the neck of a Hindu bride. A symbol of marriage and commitment.

EPILOGUE

EPILOGUE

Ibbani was turning ten. "Come on Appa! Hurry up!" she shouted as she settled in front of the desktop computer in the study. "He'd said he'll wait for me to call at 6 PM our time!"

"Amma, please keep the cake ready. I want to blow the candles in front of him," she exhorted Nitya who was giving the final touches to the cake that the two of them had baked.

I wake up in the morning
I see your face before me

I close my eyes and open them
Making sure, I'm not dreaming again

I mumble a prayer and thank the power above
All our years together in a moment flash by

A smile spreads on my face
I realise what I have in front of me

Is all that I ever wanted love to be
A constant companion, a partner in all my crimes

They'd been married for over six and a half years now. During this time, life had zipped along in the fast lane. Rishi had quickly risen through the ranks at the merged entity that had been christened Perfect Computers. He was the youngest ever member of the India Management Team. Rishi had also been featured as a part of the 'Forty under Forty' leaders list in one of the leading business magazines.

Nitya had focussed all her knowledge and her experience in evangelising computers to start a not-for-profit organisation that provided digital education.

Rishi and Nitya had both agreed that Ibbani was all they needed and decided not to have children of their own. Rishi had gone on to legally adopt Ibbani.

~

"Happy Birthday to you! Happy Birthday dear Ibby! Happy Birthday to you!" they could hear Prasanna wish Ibby over the video call.

"Amma, Appa, come quickly! Dad is online!" Ibby shouted in her excitement.

Prasanna had been faithful to his end of the bargain and had been very supportive of Rishi's decision to adopt Ibbani. Nitya and Rishi had been happy to make Prasanna an important part of Ibbani's growing up.

As she had grown older and grown in terms of inquisitiveness, Nitya and Rishi had candidly communicated with Ibbani. Not only was she aware of the slightly different context and dynamics of her family, she was comfortable with them too.

Prasanna had sent across a guitar as a birthday gift for Ibbani.

"You shouldn't have let Ibby bully you into buying one for her Sunny. The piano we bought for her last year is now a showpiece in our living room!" Rishi said joining the call as Nitya sat beside him.

"If there's one other lesson that life has taught me my dear friend," Prasanna said with a rueful smile on his face, "It is not to mess with the women who hold you in high esteem!"

DISCLAIMER AND CREDITS

All lyrics, poetry and art used are the property of the respective copyright owners.

i. *Mandya Station* sketch by **Sudham Ravinutala.**

ii. Dialogue on Page 67 borrowed from the motion picture *Sholay* (Sippy Films) written by **Salim-Javed**.

iii. *Jackpot Round* doodles by **Sudham Ravinutala.**

iv. Lyrics on Page 85 borrowed from the song *Secret* from the album *Brigade* (Capitol) by **Heart**.

v. Lyrics on Page 96 borrowed from the song *The Look* from the album *Look Sharp! (Extended Version)* (EMI) by **Roxette**.

vi. *Qutb Minar* sketch by **Sudham Ravinutala.**

vii. Lyrics on Page 161 borrowed from the song *Sona Sona* performed by *Sudesh Bhosle, Jaspinder Narula and Sonu Nigam* from the original soundtrack of the motion picture *Major Saab* (ABCL, T-Series) written and composed by **Anand Raj Anand**.

viii. *The Oratory of Our Lady of Fatima* sketch by **Sudham Ravinutala.**

ix. *Baha'i Temple* sketch by **Sudham Ravinutala.**

x. Poetry on Page 283 borrowed from the poem *Wish Come True* by **Sudham Ravinutala**.